Amy Cross is the author of more than 100 horror, paranormal, fantasy and thriller novels.

OTHER TITLES
BY AMY CROSS INCLUDE

American Coven
Annie's Room
The Ash House
Asylum
B&B
The Bride of Ashbyrn House
The Camera Man
The Curse of Wetherley House
The Devil, the Witch and the Whore
Devil's Briar
The Dog
Eli's Town
The Farm
The Ghost of Molly Holt
The Ghosts of Lakeforth Hotel
The Girl Who Never Came Back
Haunted
The Haunting of Blackwych Grange
The Night Girl
Other People's Bodies
Perfect Little Monsters & Other Stories
The Shades
The Soul Auction
Tenderling
Ward Z

Doctor Charles Grazier

The House of Jack the Ripper book 6

AMY CROSS

First published by Dark Season Books,
United Kingdom, 2017

Copyright © 2017 Amy Cross

All rights reserved. This book is a work of fiction. Names, characters, places, incidents and businesses are the product of the author's imagination or are used fictitiously. Any resemblance to actual persons, living or dead, or to actual events or locates, is entirely coincidental.

ISBN: 9781549975622

Also available in e-book format.

www.amycross.com

CONTENTS

Prologue
page 3

Chapter One
DOCTOR CHARLES GRAZIER
page 8

Chapter Two
MADDIE
page 11

Chapter Three
DOCTOR CHARLES GRAZIER
page 22

Chapter Four
MADDIE
page 30

Chapter Five
DOCTOR CHARLES GRAZIER
page 40

Chapter Six
MADDIE
page 49

Chapter Seven
DOCTOR CHARLES GRAZIER
page 56

CHAPTER EIGHT
MADDIE
PAGE 63

CHAPTER NINE
DOCTOR CHARLES GRAZIER
PAGE 70

CHAPTER TEN
MADDIE
PAGE 78

CHAPTER ELEVEN
DOCTOR CHARLES GRAZIER
PAGE 86

CHAPTER TWELVE
MADDIE
PAGE 96

CHAPTER THIRTEEN
DOCTOR CHARLES GRAZIER
PAGE 103

CHAPTER FOURTEEN
MADDIE
PAGE 112

CHAPTER FIFTEEN
DOCTOR CHARLES GRAZIER
PAGE 118

CHAPTER SIXTEEN
MADDIE
PAGE 125

CHAPTER SEVENTEEN
DOCTOR CHARLES GRAZIER
PAGE 133

CHAPTER EIGHTEEN
MADDIE
PAGE 140

CHAPTER NINETEEN
DOCTOR CHARLES GRAZIER
PAGE 146

CHAPTER TWENTY
MADDIE
PAGE 157

CHAPTER TWENTY-ONE
"DOCTOR CHARLES GRAZIER"
PAGE 164

DOCTOR CHARLES GRAZIER

THE HOUSE OF JACK THE RIPPER BOOK 6

PROLOGUE

"DOCTOR CULPEPPER CAN BE RATHER TRYING SOMETIMES, CAN HE NOT?"

Turning to Catherine, I find that she has returned to my side. She moves so gracefully through the crowd of party-goers, one can sometimes be surprised by her return. Even now, as the pianist continues to play nearby and as great works of art stand arranged for inspection along the length of the south wall, I cannot stare at anything or anybody other than my wife. She is perfect.

"The man can talk for England," she continues, rolling her eyes, "although I suppose there's no harm in that. Still, I feel dreadfully sorry for his poor wife Delilah. The young woman is scarcely able to get a word in. To live with a man like that, she must have the patience of an absolute saint."

"Then it is good that she seems to have so few words in the first place," I point out.

Catherine nudges my arm.

"Do I lie?" I continue with a faint smile. "The creature seems utterly devoid of merit. Why, I do not recall ever hearing her say anything useful in a conversation."

"Do not be so mean, Charles," Catherine says, although a smile is already crossing her lips. She is polite and diplomatic – far more so than I – and she will not admit that she agrees with my every word. "I'm sure Delilah is delightful." She pauses for a moment. "In her own way. Now if you'll excuse me, I need to find some more of these canapes before they're all taken. They're the one saving grace of this dreadful party. We shall be going home before nine, shall we not?"

"Nine?" I reply. "I was hoping to be gone by eight."

"We cannot be rude, Charles."

"I don't see why not."

"Mingle a little," she adds with a sigh. "It might actually do you some good."

As Catherine goes to fetch more canapes, I gravitate toward the far end of the room, where several of my distinguished colleagues are gathered, along with a few of the not-so-distinguished doctors from the local hospitals. Truly, I find these gatherings rather tiring, and one of the few bright sides of my impending retirement is the fact that I shall never again have to endure long, painful days with Doctors Culpepper, Markham, Shaw and all the rest. Well, not unless I bump into them at the club, anyway. Perhaps I should think about finding a *new* club.

"Having a good evening, are you?" Markham

asks languidly. "We don't often see you at these shindigs, Charles. I must say, I was rather surprised when I saw you and your dear lady wife coming in."

"One must go out occasionally," I say with a forced smile.

"The wife dragged you here, did she?" he adds.

"Of course not!" I spit back at him. "I am the man of the house!"

"Steady on," he replies, raising both eyebrows as if he's a little surprised by my tone. "I was just making a joke."

"And is that what passes for humor around here?" I ask.

"I see that your impending retirement has done little to soften your edges," Markham mutters needlessly. "Will you taking up any hobbies once you have all that spare time, or is Catherine going to be honored with your presence all day?"

"Charles and Catherine seem to prefer one another's company most of the time," Culpepper suggests. "I suppose that is to be admired." He leans closer to me. "If I had to spend too much time with Delilah, I think I would go absolutely spare. She's the perfect wife, don't get me wrong, but she is not skilled at the art of conversation." He sighs. "Then again, she has good qualities as well. I suppose I should be grateful."

As he says those words, I spot Delilah Culpepper standing near the door, and it is apparent that she is all alone. Abandoned by her husband for the evening, she has been unable to engage anybody else, and now she is simply standing meekly with an untouched glass of wine in her hand and a plate of uneaten cake. The sight is actually rather pitiful, and becomes doubly so when she attempts to speak to two women who pass by. The women ignore her, of course, and Delilah is left to go back to her silent introspection.

"Would that any of us had your perfect life," Culpepper continues, patting me on the shoulder. "Happy. Successful. Respected by all your peers. Why, I am sure that in such circumstances, anybody could be a fine man."

"And what is that supposed to mean?" I ask.

"Just that a man can be himself when he isn't tested." He pauses. "If one is tested, however, then *that* is when one discovers one's true mettle. If a man can remain strong and moral during difficult times, then I think we can surely say that he has a proper core."

"Whatever are you on about?" I reply, unable to hide the fact that I am irritated by his poor attempts at philosophy.

"I suppose I'm rambling," he admits. "You don't know how lucky you are. That's all, really."

"Charles?" a voice says suddenly, and I turn to find that Doctor Saward is approaching with some degree of urgency in his tone. "Your wife would like to see you in the drawing room," he explains. "She asked you to hurry."

I am about to tell him that I shall be along presently, when I hear the sound of Catherine coughing nearby. Immediately filled with a sense of concern, I make my excuses and hurry across the room. I tell myself that I should not overreact, and that most likely

Catherine is simply feeling tired, but then – as soon as I reach the doorway and see her bent against the table – I realize that something must be very wrong. Catherine is not a woman who allows herself to succumb to illness, nor has she ever shown even a hint of bad posture. At this moment, however, she looks positively wretched.

"Catherine?" I say cautiously, heading over to her. "I was told that you wanted to see me. Is something the matter?"

"Charles," she stammers, turning to me with blood around her lips, "what -"

Suddenly she bursts into a coughing fit. Bending over, she inadvertently sprays blood from her mouth, dappling the fine white tablecloth.

"What is wrong with me?" she gasps, sounding as if she is struggling for air. "Charles, tell me what's wrong!"

CHAPTER ONE
DOCTOR CHARLES GRAZIER

Thursday October 4th, 1888

I slip my fingers deeper into her womb, searching through the bloody mess for the child.

***

CATHERINE WAS ALWAYS SO, SO MUCH BETTER AT THIS.

Standing alone in the hallway, I peer at my reflection in the mirror and try once more to arrange my bow-tie properly. In truth, I have been struggling at this task for several minutes now, and I have tied and untied and then re-tied the damnable thing so much that I am ready to cast it aside. My hands tremble and my patience is worn thin. Yet I persist, because I want to look my best today, but also because I know how much Catherine liked me to be smart.

"You must get dressed for the street," she told me once. "If you look good, you will feel good."

"I'm not sure," I remember telling her, "that it works quite like that."

"Trust me." She smiled. "I am not letting my husband leave the house with anything other than an *immaculately* presented bow-tie."

I never learned to tie the thing properly myself, so she used to set it for me every morning, standing right in front of me in this exact spot, right up until she was too weak to even get out of bed. Even then, for a few mornings she insisted that I sat next to her while she tried to make me look acceptable. When that proved too much for her, I knew that she was feeling truly sick.

"There," I mutter finally, supposing that I have managed at least an approximation of how I should look. Lowering my hands, I see that although the bow-tie has some creases, it is at least passable. Why, I have seen men *with* wives who look worse when they arrive at the club. "That will do until Catherine is able to -"

Before I can finish, I hear a loud banging sound coming from down in the basement. The sound lasts for only a few frantic seconds, but I hold my breath for the duration, filled with a sense of overwhelming dread. The banging goes on and on and on, as if some foul force means to shake the house apart. Even when silence abruptly returns, I cannot escape the feeling that something quite dreadful must have occurred down there, and I can tell without checking that my pulse is racing. Indeed, I am also sweating rather profusely.

At least silence *has* returned, affording me another spate of calm between two storms.

"Not long now," I whisper, staring at my reflection. "Give it time to work, and soon Catherine will be back. Then everything will be alright. She will tie your..."

My voice trails off.

Am I crying?

I take a moment to dab my scratched eyes with a moist cloth. In truth, the pain and discomfort have become part of the background hum of my existence over the past few days, and I am at least comforted by the knowledge that I shall not be forced to witness that hideous perversion of Catherine on the beach. I cannot trust my mind, so my eyes must remain open. I shall attend to the problem of my lidless eyes, just as soon as Catherine is back, and for now the discomfort is my cross to bear. As I set my tinted spectacles in place, I see from my reflection that I actually look rather dapper.

With that, I make my way to the front door and prepare to step out into the world. Reaching down, I take hold of the bolt. It is a little stiff, and I have to wiggle it several times.

CHAPTER TWO
MADDIE

Today

"ALMOST GOT IT!" I call out, as I struggle once again to slide the bolt across. "Hang on..."

Suddenly it gives way, and I immediately pull the back door open. As soon as I do so, I see a look of genuine wonder on Matt's face as he stares into the house. Framed against the overgrown garden, he almost looks as if he's nervous about crossing the threshold and actually coming inside. As I wait for him to step forward, I actually start to wonder whether he might turn around and walk away.

"It's okay," I tell him. "It's just a house, right?"

I wait.

No reply.

"Right?" I ask again, although this time I can hear the tension in my own voice.

He stares into the gloomy hallway for a moment, almost as if he's in a trance, and I can't help thinking that his reaction seems similar to Jerry's yesterday. And then, just as I'm starting to wonder whether he'll start talking about weird sensations and screams that nobody else can hear, he takes a step forward and makes his way over to the center of the hallway. As he does so, the bare floorboards creak beneath his feet. They always creak, of course, but somehow they seem louder right now.

"I know what you're thinking," I continue, as I bump the door shut and walk over to join him. "We shouldn't even be here. It's private property, we're trespassing, and I know you're right. I told you I'll explain that later, but for now -"

"Wait," he says, holding up a hand as if he wants to listen more closely to the silence.

"What is it?" I ask.

Again, I wait.

Again, he says nothing.

"What?" I ask again, lowering my voice a little.

He still doesn't reply, so we stand and listen for a moment. And then, just as I'm about to tell him that I don't hear anything, I realize there *is* a very faint noise drifting up from the basement, getting a little louder and little clearer. It's not a scream, or some kind of ghost rattling its chains, but for a few seconds I struggle to realize what I'm hearing. Finally, however, the sound seems to become a little clearer, and I slowly turn to Matt as I understand the embarrassing truth.

"That's Alex and Nick," I explain, already starting to blush as sex sounds continue to rise up through the house. "I'm really sorry about them. I didn't know they'd be doing that, they're my... *friends*..."

***

"Show me what you've got here," Matt says as I step around the desk in the study and pick up one of the notebooks. "I'm due on duty in two hours, so I'm afraid I don't have much time."

"I'm sorry I called you," I reply, still blushing slightly even though we've shut the door to screen out the noises coming from the basement. "I wouldn't have, if I didn't think it was important. I mean, when you gave me your number, I really didn't mean to ever use it. Then after I called you that one time, I thought I wouldn't need to again, but -"

"Maddie."

"And I wasn't going to," I continue, speaking so fast now that I'm almost tripping over my words, "but things have gone a bit weird and I just -"

"Maddie."

"What?"

"Just calm down a little, and take your time. I'm glad you called. Now what is it that's got you all worked up like this?"

I tuck a loose strand of matted hair behind my ear as I look down at the notebook I've just opened, and as Matt comes around to join me.

My thoughts are racing, but I know that I need to settle down a little so I take a moment to figure out how I can even begin to explain all of this. I guess the best option is just to be direct.

"You said you'd researched the original Jack the Ripper," I say finally. "Well, I guess it's a huge long-shot, and it'd be an even huger coincidence, but some of the things we've found in this house seem like they might be connected. To Jack the Ripper, I mean." Hesitating, I realize that these words sound ridiculous, but I guess I need to explain. "Look at these diagrams," I add, pointing at some of the sketches. "They were drawn by a guy named Doctor Charles Grazier, who lived in this house right around the time Jack the Ripper was active."

"I've never heard that name before," he mutters. "These sketches are... kind of freaky."

"I mean, they're anatomical, right?" I continue.

"Definitely." He sounds as if I've caught his attention.

"Some of them look like he was planning experiments," I point out, "or at least operations."

I wait for Matt to reply, but he simply reaches down and turns to the next page.

"Some of them are kinda gross," I continue. "I don't really know much about the state of medicine back in the 1880's, but it looks like he was getting up to some pretty extreme stuff."

Again I wait, but Matt simply turns to another page.

"These are very detailed and interesting drawings," he says finally, "but I'm sure there might be good reasons why someone would be working on them. It doesn't mean that he was actually the killer."

"Okay, but look at *this*," I add, leafing through the pages until I find the picture of the woman with the torn-open belly. "Look at the name."

"Maddie..."

"Look at the name!"

"It looks like..." He pauses, clearly struggling to read the handwriting. "Delilah? Delilah Culpepper?"

"The woman from the alley."

I wait for him to tell me I'm crazy, that I'm finding patterns that don't exist, but instead he turns the notebook a little so that he can better try to decipher the comments. He seems genuinely fascinated, and I can feel a slowly, growing sense of anticipation in the pit of my belly as I start to realize that maybe we've stumbled onto something after all.

A moment later he turns to the next page, then the next, and I can tell that he's starting to take this seriously.

"Well?" I ask finally. "Do you think it could mean something? Or is it just a load of coincidences?"

Again I wait, but again he seems utterly engrossed. This time I don't disturb him, and I wait until he's checked several more pages.

When he eventually turns to me again, I can see that he's not going to dismiss this as pure speculation.

"You said this Grazier guy was a doctor," he says cautiously.

"He had this, like, operating theater down in the basement. I'll show you, when my friends are, uh... finished."

"What kind of operating theater?"

"There's a slab in the middle of the room, with gutters that I think are for draining blood away. There's also a load of old surgical equipment." I pause for a moment, worried that maybe I sound crazy. "I mean, it's possible that there's a simple explanation for that, right? Maybe he just liked working from home? Maybe back then it was totally normal to have an operating theater in your basement?"

"No," he replies, "I don't think that quite cuts it."

"There are more notebooks," I explain, starting to feel as if I'm being useful. "I gave some of them to the guy who lives next door. He's been researching the house, he knows a lot about its history and about the people who lived here. I'm not certain, but I think maybe he's got his suspicions about Doctor Grazier as well."

"I'd very much like to speak to him."

"And there are other weird things," I add. "Like a knife hanging from a tree in the garden, and some of the details about Doctor Grazier's life. He had a wife who was sick, and she disappeared around the time of the Jack the Ripper killings. Clearly Grazier knew Delilah Culpepper, and Delilah's husband Thomas also disappeared. Then there's the fact that Grazier committed suicide, right after the last of the confirmed Jack the Ripper murders. And there are the letters."

"Letters?"

"We found old letters," I continue, "and we think they might have been drafts of the letters that were sent to the newspapers. Like the famous 'From Hell' letter, things like that. It's almost like he was practicing before he sent them out."

"And you have those here in the house?"

"I can show you all of it." I pause again. "Do you think we might be onto something?"

"I've been looking into the Delilah Culpepper case," he continues. "A few days after she was found dead, her body was stolen from the mortuary. She was due to undergo a second examination, but somebody broke in during the night and she was never seen again."

"So she and her husband *both* vanished?" I point out.

He nods. "What about supernatural activity?"

"I'm sorry?"

"There'd be ghosts here." He looks past me, watching the far side of the room with eager concern. "If this is the house of Jack the Ripper, then people most likely died within these walls. There would have been misery and pain here, and so much suffering. People screaming and crying out as they suffered the most unimaginable pain. I find it very difficult to believe that all of that misery wouldn't result in some serious supernatural presences. Of all the places in London, this would have to be one of the most likely to suffer hauntings." He turns to me. "Have you seen or felt any ghosts here, Maddie?"

"Well, I..." My voice trails off for a moment as I realize that he's serious. "I don't know that I exactly believe in ghosts..."

"But have there been things? Things you've maybe dismissed?"

"I..." Again, I can't quite figure out how to reply, but finally I realize that maybe I should just be honest.

"Yeah," I tell him, "sure. There have been things I've kind of ignored because they seemed a little weird. I've... seen a few things. I heard a bell."

"And you've felt the atmosphere in this place, right?"

"Atmosphere?"

"I felt it as soon as I got close to the house, and then it got much stronger when you opened the door and I came inside. It was like a barrier, like something physical that marked the door, almost as if it was trying to keep me out. I'm not joking, I had to really force myself to come inside after you opened that door. There's something here, Maddie. It's so powerful, it's almost overwhelming. Are you seriously telling me that you *don't* feel it?"

"I just feel a little cold," I reply, although I'm a little freaked out by the fact that he sounds a lot like Jerry right now. "It's an empty, slightly damp old house."

"That's not right," he mutters, staring at me. "It's so strong. Why don't you feel it?"

Lost for words, I simply shrug.

"And you've spent nights here?" he continues. "Alone?"

I nod.

"You weren't scared?"

"It was too busy to be scared," I tell him. "Too cold. I was kind of hurt, too."

"And nothing happened?"

"Little noises. Creaks, things like that. But nothing crazy."

"Then the presence must know about you," he adds. "It's aware of all of us, but it must be *particularly* aware of *you*. It must be strong, so it could have reached out to you if it wanted. That means it's choosing to leave you alone instead, although I think maybe there's more than one thing here. The feeling is so powerful, I wouldn't be surprised if there are two or three very strong presences, and maybe several others that aren't quite as forceful. Either way, there has to be a reason why you're oblivious."

"I don't know," I tell him, although I'm starting to feel a little concerned by the fact that he's so certain. I would never have guessed that Matt's this willing to accept the idea of ghosts. "I'm just telling you, I don't feel anything here. Apart from the first night, nothing strange has happened."

"The first night?"

Sighing, I realize that maybe it's best to open up to him. I try to figure out how to explain what happened, but then I figure I should just show him.

"I was hurt when I got here," I explain, as I start lifting the side of my shirt a little. "It was even before I met you. Don't overreact, but I'd been stabbed. A little."

As soon as my shirt is above the wound, I see that the stitches are still in place and that the inflammation is barely visible.'

Still, the whole thing looks pretty gruesome, and I can already tell that I won't be able to play this off as simply being nothing. I watch as Matt reaches out to touch the stitches, but he holds back and then moves his hand away.

I'm about to tell him that it's healed a lot, but I guess maybe that would just make him worry more.

"Exactly what happened here?" he asks.

"It's nothing, I just -"

"Maddie, tell me!" he says firmly. "This is not nothing. What happened to you?"

"I just got followed one night, in the street."

"By who?"

"I don't know. I didn't see his face."

"And he attacked you?"

"I got away!"

"Why didn't you mention this the other night?"

"I didn't want to make a fuss," I explain. "I thought you'd get funny about it. And as you can tell, I'm fine. It healed by itself. Well, not by itself, but I think I stitched myself up."

"You stitched yourself up?" he asks incredulously.

"Sure." Taking a deep breath, I can't help thinking that I must sound completely insane. "People can do stuff like that, right?" I continue. "When they're in a bad way, they can do things they can't do usually. So I figured that's what it was, and I just..."

My voice trails off as I start to realize how crazy that sounds. Then again, if I didn't stitch my own would, who saved me?

"Maddie," Matt says cautiously, "I think -"

Suddenly the door swings open, banging hard against the wall and revealing Alex and Nick staring at us.

"Hey!" Nick yells angrily. "Maddie, what's

to prove to myself that I can move through the world without anybody noticing my affliction. Now, however, I am momentarily a little concerned.

"I am quite alright," I say cautiously, stopping so that the doorman can take my coat. As he does so, I adjust me spectacles to make absolutely certain that my damaged eyes cannot be seen. "I am afraid I have simply been far too busy to come to the club."

"Well, I can't argue with that," Markham says with a smile. "Not everyone can spend their days in idleness, sitting around here reading the newspapers. You're not like the rest of us, Doctor Grazier, are you?"

"I suppose not," I reply, making my way over to where Doctors Markham and Shaw are enjoying a glass of brandy over lunch. I suppose I should have known that they would be here.

"Aren't you going to take those spectacles off?" Doctor Markham asks, peering up at me. "They're tinted awfully dark."

"A mere precaution to fend off headaches," I explain, as I reach up and adjust the spectacles to ensure that they completely cover my damaged eyes. At the same time, I am continually rotating my eyeballs as much as possible, to moisten them and alleviate – as much as possible – the sensation of dust and scratches. "You must excuse me if I seem rude."

"Not at all, old boy." Markham turns to Shaw. "Don't you think Doctor Grazier actually might start a new fashion?"

He waits, but Doctor Shaw is engrossed in a newspaper, and I cannot help but notice that the headline concerns another murder supposedly committed by Jack the Ripper. I was not out last night, of course, so any murder must have been committed by somebody else, but it seems that the newspaper industry is rather keen to promote the idea that a madman is wandering the streets at night. This Jack the Ripper craze seems to be about 5% rooted in truth, and 95% concocted as a means to sell lies to the unsuspecting and gormless populace. I suppose the general fuss and bother is a useful smokescreen, making it somewhat easier for the true facts to remain concealed.

"Huh?" Doctor Shaw says suddenly, glancing at us as if he has only just realized that we are here. "Did somebody say something?"

"You must forgive him," Markham tells me with a chuckle. "The old fool has become utterly fixated upon the foul details of these murders. A week or so ago, it was only the women who were taken up with the matter, but now the whole thing seems to be spreading further and further up the chain of civilization. Why, at this rate, they'll soon be nattering about the killer at the palace!"

"A lady of the night was found in Watchworth Road," Shaw says keenly, his eyes wide with horror. "They say her head had been cut cleanly away, and that various unpleasant things had been done to her nether regions. Things that are too gruesome to publish."

"Some of the details that one hears," Markham adds, "are quite alarming. One barely dares read what he's been doing to his victims, yet at the same time one cannot look away. This Jack the Ripper fellow must be completely out of his mind. He can't possibly be English, of course. Somebody like that can only have been imported from some wretched, far-flung corner of the world." He takes a sip from his glass. "Foreigners," he adds under his breath.

"At least he most likely won't strike tonight," Shaw replies.

"And why is that?" I ask.

"Apparently he very rarely attacks on Thursdays," he continues. "I don't know who worked it out, but for some reason the police and everybody else seem to believe that Thursdays are comparatively safe. Not that there haven't been murders in the middle of the week, of course, but still it seems that there might be a pattern. I say, perhaps the killer has a recurring engagement on Thursday evenings. Do you think anybody has thought of that? Might it be worth my dropping around to Scotland Yard with the suggestion?"

"I'm sure the police don't need help from the likes of us," Markham says with a smile.

"They don't seem to be doing a very good job as it is!" Shaw protests. "I'd say they're probably rather desperate! We'll see, but I imagine the killer won't strike tonight."

"I would not wager any money on that idea," I tell him, amused by the idea that these fools think the streets will be safe tonight. "Indeed, I have a very strong feeling that there *will* be a murder tonight. Call it a hunch, if you will, but I would be very surprised if some lady of the night is not found dead when the sun rises tomorrow morning."

Even if I have to commit the deed, purely to

show the fellow that he is wrong.

"Really?" Shaw asks. "What makes you think that? Have you been following the newspaper reports as well?"

"Hardly," I mutter, making my way over to the bar, where a drink is already waiting for me. "This Jack the Ripper individual is clearly a man of great intelligence and skill," I explain, taking a sip from the glass and then turning to them. My eyes are burning, but of course I can no longer blink. "Why, I dare say that he might very well be a more skilled surgeon than half the men who currently practice in the hospitals of this great city."

"You cannot be serious!" Markham splutters.

"London is awash with charlatans and criminals," I explain, "but this Ripper man is most certainly a cut above."

"But the newspapers -"

"Dash the newspapers!" I announce. "Why, I'd even say that they are *worse* than the killer himself. At least there is a chance that he has a noble cause, whereas those newspaper men are merely making a profit from the murders."

"It *is* the talk of the town," Shaw points out, sounding a little deflated.

"Fortunately I am not replying solely upon the newspapers for my information," I continue, cutting him off before he can issue some new and undoubtedly vapid opinion. "It might interest you to learn, gentlemen, that I myself have been called in to assist the police. Why, I spent a great deal of time advising Inspector Sanderson of Scotland Yard about the murders."

"You *did*?" Markham says, clearly shocked as both he and Shaw lean forward in their chairs. "Did you see any of the bodies?"

"I saw all of them," I reply dismissively, with a wave of my hand. "Honestly, gentlemen, that in itself was hardly anything. Many of the supposed Ripper victims were in fact killed by lowly copycats who lacked the real killer's grace and finesse. As I walked through that room of corpses, I could instantly tell which had been murdered by the real Jack the Ripper, and which had been merely slaughtered by one of his artless followers."

"And you *saw* the victims?" Markham asks. "You actually saw them with your own eyes?"

"My dear fellow," I reply, adjusting my spectacles once again, "I examined some of them very closely indeed."

"How?" Shaw asks indignantly. "What I mean is, why would they ask *you* to look at the bodies, rather than -"

"Rather than *you*?" I say with a faint smile. "I can only assume that it was *my* expertise that they required, that they deemed me to be the most reliable expert witness. Perhaps word reached them about my prowess. I can't help it if people talk about me."

At this, the two men turn to one another, and it's clear that they're equally startled. Markham and Shaw have both, over the years, given subtle indications that they believe themselves to be my superiors, that they in some manner begrudge my every success. Now it seems that they are having trouble wrapping their heads around the idea that the police came to me for assistance, and I cannot deny that I am highly amused by this development. Both men are positively oozing resentment.

Finally, Markham turns to me.

"Can we come next time?" he asks plaintively.

"I beg your pardon?" I reply.

"Can you take us? Next time the police ask for your help, I mean. Would it be possible for you to let us come with you, to see the bodies? We wouldn't say anything. We'd just stand behind you and... look..."

"For research purposes, of course," Shaw adds. "To aid our understanding."

"Please," Markham continues. "I'll do anything you want in return. I'll even pay you!"

"I rather think that will not be possible," I tell the gentlemen. "When I was asked to help, I was told that everything was to be kept in the strictest confidence. As you will no doubt understand, the police are rather keen to avoid turning these murders into a spectacle."

"Of course, of course," Markham nods, before hesitating for a moment. "Still, if they *do* want another opinion, would you be so kind as to pass them my contact details?"

"And mine!" Shaw says keenly.

"I shall do what I can," I reply, "but please, do not expect much. After all, this is a serious murder investigation, not some freak show for the masses. The police are hardly likely to invite people in to see such gruesome corpses, not unless they believe that they have something to gain."

"Quite right," Shaw grumbles, sinking back into his chair and clearly feeling rather aggrieved. "One only wished to offer one's help, that is all. One likes to contribute to society when one can."

"Are you sure you're alright?" Markham asks, still staring at me. "No offense, old chap, but those spectacles look awfully funny when you wear them inside. Can't you take them off, not even for a moment?"

"Alas not," I reply, forcing a smile. "I must keep them on at all times. I am afraid to say that I have had rather an unusual twenty-four hours. Indeed, if I were to tell you everything that has happened to me, I am quite sure that you would never believe a word."

"Too busy running around helping the police?" Shaw mutters, his tone positively dripping with resentment and irritation. "Well, I'm sure that's alright for some. I'm glad that you have a hobby."

"Indeed," I reply, "and in actual fact, I have been asked to visit Scotland Yard again today. It seems that the esteemed Inspector Sanderson requires my help yet again." I take another sip from my glass. "And really, when the city of London is suffering through its darkest hour, how could I possibly refuse?"

CHAPTER FOUR
MADDIE

Today

"THIS IS INCREDIBLE," Matt says as he steps across the basement and stops to look at the slab in the middle of the room. "I can't believe what I'm seeing."

"You're *so* dead!" Alex whispers into my ear from behind. "If this puts our payday in danger, I swear you're dead! We told you not to invite anyone else into the house!"

"We need to show it to other people," I reply, keeping my voice down. "We're not -"

Suddenly she nudges my arm hard.

"We'll talk about this later," she says darkly. "I can't believe you, Maddie. I thought we were all on the same side."

Ignoring her, I make my way over to the slab, stopping opposite Matt and reaching down to run my hands across the grooves. It's strange to think about what must have happened down here more than a century ago, and for a moment I can't help imagining some poor woman tied to the slab while her guts are torn open. I keep telling myself that I'm being dramatic, that nothing quite so lurid took place in this dank and cold room, but at the same time I can't help noticing the dark stains that run along some of the grooves.

"I think these are part of a drainage system," I explain, "taking the blood away. If you look closely, you can even see something left over. Blood, maybe. There are scalpels and saws and things over on the bench behind you, and even what look like old pieces of rope."

He turns and looks over at the counter, and then he starts walking away from the slab. Just as I think he's about to take a look at the knives, however, he heads past them and stops to take a closer look at the far wall. He's been lost in thought for a while now, saying very little, and I desperately want to know what he thinks. Part of me wants him to tell me this whole thing is ridiculous, and the rest of me wants him to say that this really *is* the house of Jack the Ripper.

"Those symbols are in other parts of the house too," I tell him, "but I don't think they mean anything."

I wait, but he doesn't reply.

"Do they?" I ask finally.

"Of course they mean something," he says, reaching out and running a hand over the roughly-carved shapes. "There are a lot of them, and they're very intricate. Whoever put them here clearly believed that they were going to do *something*. I've seen things like this before, in books about the occult. Not *exactly* the same, of course, but not a million miles away either. Whether they actually worked or not is one thing, but they undoubtedly meant something to whoever put them here."

"So here's the thing," Alex says suddenly, as she and Nick come over to join me next to the slab. "We've got this whole situation in hand, so we don't need any help from outsiders. Maddie was obviously just seeking a fourth opinion from you, whoever you are, but there's nothing for you to do here. You really just need to hightail it out of here and keep your mouth shut. You're not getting a penny."

He turns to her, clearly surprised by her attitude.

"We're not paying you off," she adds. "Maybe, like, 5%, but no more."

"This isn't about money," he says cautiously. "This is a crime scene. It *was*, anyway, and I still want to get it checked out in case there's any link to what's happening at the moment."

"You don't get to decide when we tell people about this," Alex replies. "That's our decision to make, thanks very much."

He shakes his head. "The police -"

"We'll call the police when we're good and ready," she adds.

"I'm a police *officer*," he replies.

She opens her mouth to dismiss him, but then I see the shock in her eyes. "You're *what*?" she stammers, before glancing at me with daggers. "He's a *what*, Maddie? Did you know this?"

"I'm a police officer," he says again, stepping back toward us, "and as of this moment, this entire house is a potential crime scene. That means I'm going to be calling in reinforcements, and it means you three all have to get out of here and make yourself available for questioning. I'm also going to need to know *exactly* what you've touched, and what you might have disturbed, and we'll need to get prints and samples from all of you so we can eliminate -"

"Hang on!" Alex says, holding her hands up as she steps toward him. "Let's backtrack a little. You're a cop?"

Reaching into his pocket, Matt pulls out a small black wallet and opens it, revealing his police ID.

"Nice," Alex says darkly, turning and casting another dagger-filled glare straight at me. "When you screw up, Maddie, you really go all the way, don't you? I mean, you really are a piece of work."

"I had to call him," I tell her. "Come on, be serious for a moment. We couldn't just sit on this indefinitely. We had to get help!"

"I'm going to call for back-up," Matt says, slipping past us and heading to the door that leads back up into the hallway. He checks his phone, but evidently he can't get any signal down here. "I need the three of you to wait here until that back-up arrives, and then we're going to figure out exactly what's going on here."

"That's not fair!" Nick calls after him. "We're the ones who solved this!"

"And you'll get all the credit you deserve," Matt adds, before hurrying up the steps.

"We want more than credit!" Nick adds, before turning and scowling at me. "Good job, short-ass. Do you wanna stab us both in the back while you're at it?"

"And what exactly was *your* plan?" I ask.

"My plan was pretty brilliant, actually," he snarls, stepping toward me. "My plan was going to make us all goddamn millionaires!"

He reaches for my neck, but Alex pushes him away.

"You can't be on her side!" he sneers at her. "She's put everything in jeopardy!"

"Let's just figure this out," she says cautiously. "It's not the end of the world, just 'cause one cop has shown up."

"I did what I had to," I reply, before turning and hurrying after Matt. "I'm sorry."

"Get back here!" Nick snarls. "We're not done with you!"

I mutter something about going to check something, but I don't look back. Heading up the stairs, I reach the hallway just in time to see Matt walking out through the back door.

He already has his phone in his hands and he's holding it out as if he's still trying to get some signal.

"Hey, wait up!" I call out, rushing to catch up to him.

"I don't have time," he replies. "Maddie, this could really help us."

"I'm sorry I dragged you into it all," I tell him. "I'm sure you already had a million things to do."

"No, I'm glad you called," he replies, turning to

me. He hesitates for a moment, and then his features soften just a little. "You needed to call someone. Besides, I was worried about you."

"Worried? Why?"

"Maybe not *worried*, exactly," he adds. "I mean, I was... I was just thinking about you. A lot. Well, not thinking about you, more..."

His voice trails off, as if he's not quite sure what to say.

"I just noticed that I hadn't heard from you," he adds finally. "I was wondering if you were okay. Last time we spoke, you seemed really out of it, as if you were hallucinating. You sounded really sick, Maddie."

"I'm okay now."

"Are you sure?"

I nod.

"I've been kicking myself for not doing more to help," he continues. "The streets are still on lock-down and I know you won't go to one of the centers, but I should have offered to let you stay at my place. I can take the sofa-bed and you can have my room."

"You don't need to do that," I tell him.

"Where else are you going to go?"

"I'll be fine."

"You sure can't stay here," he replies. "Maddie, we'll talk about this later, but right now I have to make a phone call and get some back-up here. The odds of this place being linked to the current murders is low, but the timing of it all makes me uneasy, okay? Just stay put, stay safe, and wait until I get back." He checks his phone. "There's no signal here. I'll have to try out in the street."

"I'll get the notebooks together," I reply, figuring that I can at least be useful. "I already gave some to Jerry next door, but I'm sure he'll be happy to turn them over to you."

As Matt heads outside to search for cellphone signal, I make my way into the study.

Rushing to the desk, I start gathering together all the notebooks and letters. My mind is racing and I can't think straight, but I know that I have to help Matt. Frankly, I can't believe I didn't call him sooner, but at least this mess is going to get sorted out now.

Alex and Nick were getting totally carried away, thinking we could handle this ourselves. They'll have to admit that I'm right eventually, once their anger has died down, and I'm sure they'll still be able to make some money out of the whole situation.

I'll even donate my share of anything, so they have more to split.

"You've really done it this time, Maddie."

Startled, I look over at the doorway and see that Alex is watching me with an expression of pure, stony-faced anger.

"Please," I stammer, "try to understand, I only did what I thought was -"

"You stupid little bitch," she continues. "Since the day I met you, I've done nothing but try to help you, and *this* is how you repay me? If it wasn't for me, Maddie, you'd be dead by now."

"I'm only -"

"You'd be dead!" she yells, stepping toward me.

"Do you have any idea how pathetic and vulnerable you looked when you arrived in London? If I hadn't taken you under my wing, you'd have ended up getting snatched and taken somewhere by some really bad people, and do you -"

"Alex, please..."

"And do you know how the cops would have eventually found you? You'd probably have ended up dead in some abandoned warehouse, face-down in the dirt with your pants around your ankles and blood smeared around every orifice. You would've died in fear and agony. People like you do *not* survive on the streets, Maddie, but I took a liking to you and I kept you safe. And now, after all that, this is how you pay me back? Seriously? You sad, ungrateful little cow!"

"You did so much for me," I reply, "and I'll never forget that, but I had to do the right thing."

"You've ruined our big chance!"

"No, I -"

"You're a double-crossing little bitch," she adds, "and I will never, ever forgive you for trying to destroy our one shot at making it off the streets. I was actually starting to defend you to Nick, but then he made me realize that you've completely betrayed us. He made me realize that we're going to have to start doing things completely his way from now on."

"I only -"

"And I will make sure," she sneers, coming even closer until she's right on the other side of the desk, staring at me with pure hatred, "that you get left so far behind, we won't even hear your sad little voice when you're *begging* us to help you. Because when this is all over, Nick and I are going to be set for the rest of our lives, and you – at best – will go back to starving to death on the streets."

"Alex -"

"Because guess what? You're still the same sniveling little runt I first met, and you won't last out there. And when one day I hear that you were found naked and tied up and dead, just some bloated corpse that was weighed down in a lake after some gang had their way with you, I swear to God I'll raise a glass of champagne and have a laugh at the thought of your miserable death. And if anyone even bothers to give you a proper grave, I promise I'll come and find it some day and piss all over it!"

"I have to take these," I mutter, feeling tears in my eyes as I gather the rest of the notebooks up and start making my way around the desk. "I'm sorry. I'm really, really sorry. I have to go and help Matt now."

"I don't think so," she says darkly.

"It's too late," I point out as I head toward the door. "You can't stop me. I couldn't undo the fact that I told him, even if I wanted to. And I don't!"

"Maddie!"

Sighing, I turn to her. "Alex -"

Suddenly she punches me, hitting me hard in the jaw and sending me thudding back against the wall. All the notebooks fall from my hands, clattering down onto the floorboards.

Letting out a gasp of pain, I barely have time to even realize what's happening before she comes at me again. This time she hits me on the side of the temple, striking me so hard that I instantly lose consciousness and slump to the floor.

CHAPTER FIVE
DOCTOR CHARLES GRAZIER

Thursday October 4th, 1888

Blood dribbles between my fingers.

***

"THIS IS HER," Sanderson says as he pulls a sheet away, revealing the bloodless, naked body of a young woman. "As I told you, this one's not quite as old as the others. I know that shouldn't make it any worse, but..."

He hesitates for a moment.

"By all accounts she was a good, quiet girl," he adds finally. "Not like the street-walkers who usually end up in here. This one was barely a woman at all."

"Indeed not," I reply, adjusting my glasses a little as I look down at the corpse. "I can tell you right away, however, that this is *not* one of the Ripper's victims."

"Are you sure?"

"How could anyone mistake this for his work?" I ask, stepping around the table and taking a closer look at the belly area. The girl's stomach has been torn open and some cretin has gouged her insides away, but the work is sloppy and aimless. "This person clearly had no understanding of basic human anatomy," I explain, reaching down and pointing at what remains of the liver. "Look how this section has been hacked repeatedly. Why would anybody do that? There's nothing here but sheer, psychopathic barbarity."

"Why would anybody do *any* of this?" he asks. "Jack the Ripper must be mad anyway, so why -"

"Of course he's not mad!" I snap, turning to him. "Do you seriously persist with this foolish notion? The man is clearly a genius! Whoever killed this girl, perhaps *he* is afflicted by some form of insanity, but the real Jack the Ripper is quite clearly a man of calm brilliance!"

I wait for a reply, but now Sanderson is simply staring at me, as if he's in some way surprised by what I have told him. I honestly fail to understand how anybody could rise to such a high position within the police service, without gaining at least a sliver of common sense.

"A girl disappeared near your home recently," he says after a moment.

"I beg your pardon?"

"A girl disappeared. Vanished from an alley while she was working."

"How would I know anything about that?" I ask.

"I saw you at your window," he continues. "I was sent to speak to some potential witnesses, and I saw you watching from your house. You must have seen me too."

"I do not believe so."

"You looked straight at me."

"I imagine," I say with a sigh, "that I simply wondered what was causing the commotion. I live in a very genteel part of the city, you know, and it's quite unfortunate when large crowds gather in the vicinity. Most likely, I felt the whole thing to be rather common and I -"

"Are your eyes alright, Doctor Grazier?"

"My eyes?"

"Those spectacles," he mutters, keeping his gaze fixed on me, "are rather dark."

"They're designed to reduce the instance of headaches," I tell him.

"I didn't know that such things existed."

"Well, you have learned something, have you not?" I reply, starting to feel more than a little restless. "Now is there anything else that you wanted to ask me, or might I be allowed to go on my way? I have a great deal to get done today, and my time is too valuable to be wasted on trivial matters. Why your own doctors cannot tell you these things, I cannot possibly understand."

"There's one more thing," he says, turning and heading to a door in the far corner. "Please, I know you're a very busy man, but I'd like your expert opinion on one more case. Just one."

Sighing, I realize that I should probably indulge

the moron a little longer. Making my way toward the door, I cannot help thinking that this entire visit is a waste of time, and it's hard to believe that this Sanderson fellow has the temerity to ask for my help on such a regular basis. Indeed, it seems to me that Scotland Yard is run in a rather haphazard manner, and I'm minded to raise the matter next time I chance upon the commissioner at a social gathering.

"Do you go out a lot at night?" Sanderson asks, holding the door open for me as I step through into the next room.

"What does that have to do with anything?"

"I just wondered. A man of your status and wealth must be invited to many places. And even if you don't like crowds, perhaps you simply enjoy walking the streets of the city?"

He leads me through another set of doors.

"Lately my wife has been ill," I snap, "and -"

Stopping suddenly, I see Delilah Culpepper's dead body laid out naked on a table. There is no reason why this should disturb me, of course, yet I feel some unaccountable sense of concern as I take a step closer and see the woman's glassy eyes staring straight up toward the ceiling. Her skin is greatly discolored compared to how she appeared the other day, when I deposited her body in an alley far from my home, but it is most certainly her nonetheless.

"Delilah Culpepper," Sanderson says, standing behind me. "Did you know her, Doctor Grazier?"

"No," I reply, "of course not."

"Are you sure? You were close to her husband,

Doctor Thomas Culpepper."

I turn to the man. "None of which means that I paid any attention to his wife. Besides, Culpepper and I were acquaintances, at best. We merely drank at the same club for a period."

"Thomas Culpepper has not been seen for two days," he replies. "We were asked by members of his family to seek out any information concerning him, and just a few hours later his wife's body was found in an alley called Gregson Way. As you can see, she's in a pretty bad state."

"How unfortunate," I mutter.

"I had somebody take a look at her already," he continues. "Unfortunate doesn't quite cover everything that happened to her. For one thing, her heart and liver and kidneys are missing, and the procedure seems to have been carried out by somebody with surgical knowledge. Not, however, in the alley where she was found. One of our doctors is convinced that she was killed somewhere else and merely dumped in that location. For another thing, I'm told that it's likely a child was cut from her womb. That's not something that the Ripper of Whitechapel has done before."

"I had no idea that the Culpeppers were expecting a child," I reply.

"It wasn't very far advanced," he says, stepping around to the other side of the table and looking down at Delilah's body. "Poor little thing, just starting to grow and then torn from is mother. Oh, and Delilah had been almost entirely drained of blood as well. It's all very shocking, but it definitely seems to match the key hallmarks of the Ripper case. Tell me, Doctor Grazier, do you think that Delilah Culpepper was killed by the man they're calling Jack the Ripper?"

"How would I know?"

"You were quick to give your opinion a moment ago," he replies. "Why not now?"

Looking down at Delilah's ravaged belly, I pretend to consider the matter for a moment. My mind is racing, and I cannot determine whether or not it would be advantageous for me to confirm the idiot's idea. After a few seconds, however, I realize that I only have one choice if I am to protect myself.

"No," I say finally, "I do not see many similarities. Not at all. A cursory glance is enough to convince me that this woman was carved open by a -"

Stopping suddenly, I realize that perhaps I am being a little hasty. After all, I worked long and hard on Delilah Culpepper the other night, and I was very careful to ensure that I removed her child and her organs with my usual delicacy. To deny this would perhaps seem suspicious, even to a man as simple as Sanderson, so I quickly decide that I should try a different approach. Indeed, this situation might even prove useful.

"Actually, yes," I say, trying to sound convincing, "perhaps this poor woman *was* killed by somebody with a little more skill. Now that I look a little more closely, I see some cuts that suggest the work of an individual with a great degree of experience. Indeed, the more I consider the matter, the more I see this evidence. I think I can confidently state that Ms. Culpepper was killed by a surgeon. She is almost certainly another victim of Jack the Ripper. You can tell your newspaper friends to print that, if they like."

"Fascinating," Sanderson says, keeping his eyes fixed on me. "A surgeon, you say?"

"Or somebody who gained the skills some other way."

I wait for him to come up with some fresh point of idiocy, but instead he is simply watching me with a strange expression on his face. In fact, it looks very much as if the man is engaged in deep thought, which I imagine is quite unusual for him and perhaps even a little uncomfortable. Still, I would prefer him to stop looking at me in such a strange manner, and I am minded to tell him that he is making me feel troubled.

"I think I know who did this," he says suddenly.

"I beg your pardon?"

"The Ripper," he continues, still watching me closely from the other side of the table. "It's just a hunch, and I have no evidence, but a name occurs to me. Indeed, I am quite surprised that it did not occur to me earlier. The truth would seem to be right in front of my eyes."

He lets out a gasp of frustration.

"How could I have been so foolish?" he asks. "Sometimes I wonder whether I am even fit for this job. The truth has been staring at me and I have remained entirely ignorant."

"I'm sure I have no idea what you mean," I reply, and now my throat feels very dry. Reaching up, I adjust my spectacles. "Perhaps I should leave you alone to get on with your work. I myself have several engagements to which I must attend this afternoon."

"Please don't take offense at what I'm about to say," he continues, "but I think it is clear now that the murderer is a skilled surgeon and a madman to boot, and there is only one name that fits the bill." He hesitates again, and I cannot help but feel that with his gaze he is attempting to peel back some aspect of my nature. "Or am I wrong?" he whispers. "I don't think I am, but if you have some kind of counterpoint to offer, then now would be the time to do so. Doctor Grazier, I don't have any evidence right now, but that'll come. A day, two at most, and I'll be able to tell the world. I'll be able to reveal the true identity of Jack the Ripper."

"I..."

My voice trails off. Has this simple fellow stumbled upon the truth?

"That is to say," I manage finally, "the idea is preposterous. If you are seriously suggesting -"

"Doctor Thomas Culpepper is the Ripper," he continues, interrupting me.

I open my mouth again, to protest my innocence, but at the very last moment I realize what he said.

"Did you suspect?" he asks, tilting his head slightly. "You know the man, do you not? Did you truly not suspect him at all?"

Shocked to my core, and also desperately relieved, all I can manage is to slowly shake my head.

"Good," he continues, "because if you *had* suspected, and if you still had said nothing to the police, I might have considered charging you with obstruction. I'm sorry, Doctor Grazier, I know Doctor Culpepper is a trusted colleague of yours, but the facts are the facts. Now the man is missing, and his wife is dead on this table between us, and I don't think anybody can seriously doubt the truth anymore."

He takes a step back and looks down at Delilah's corpse.

"Doctor Thomas Culpepper," he adds finally, "is the man they call Jack the Ripper."

CHAPTER SIX
MADDIE

Today

SUDDENLY AN INTENSE PAIN BURSTS THROUGH MY BODY.

Letting out an anguished gasp, I lunge forward and open my eyes, only to feel my wrists pull tight against two coiled ropes as I see Alex leaning toward me and grinning. I instinctively pull again, barely able to work out where I am, but the ropes pull again. I keep pulling filled with panic, until I look at Alex again and feel a sudden, cold stillness press against my chest.

"So where did this come from, huh?" she asks, looking down at my waist. "Looks nasty."

Before I even have a chance to realize what she means, I feel the pain reach a new intensity. I cry out again, but this time I can tell that something's tugging against the stitches in my waist. As the pain continues, I manage to look down and see that Alex has slipped the tip of her little finger under a section of the stitches, and that fresh blood is running from the wound as she continues to pull. I try to twist away, but this only makes the pain worse as her fingertip pulls against the very edge of the stitches, tearing at my sore skin.

"Don't worry," she says finally, letting go and sitting back. "I'm not a total bitch. I'll leave them in. I just wondered how you got them, that's all."

Whimpering with pain, I try yet again to pull away from her, only to find that I'm on the cold stone floor in the basement. Looking up, I see to my horror that my wrists are tied to two thick lengths of rope, which in turn have been passed around one of the stone columns near the slab. I pull hard, until my wrists start to chafe, but it's already clear that there's no way to get free. Between the column and the ropes and my shoulders, the weakest link is definitely my shoulders, which means I'd have tear my arms out of their sockets in order to get free.

"It's not forever," Alex explains, still kneeling in front of me as she wipes my blood from her fingers, smearing it first against the floor and then against the fabric of my trousers. "Nick and I couldn't let you ruin this for us, so we've had to take you out of the equation for a little while. It wasn't my idea, it was his, but he really talked me round. Don't even bother calling for help, either, 'cause no-one'll hear you. Not down here." She pauses, before leaning closer. "We're not going to do anything permanent to you, okay? It's just while we get our shit straight. So if I were you, I'd stop panicking and just wait it out."

"What are you doing?" I stammer, pulling again and again on the ropes. "Alex, let me out of here!"

She sighs. "Did you not hear a word I just told you."

"Alex, please!" I sob, still pulling even though I know it's fruitless. "Alex, we're friends, you can't tie me up like this!"

"We *were* friend," she replies coldly, "until you screwed me over. Nick helped me to see that."

"Alex, I'm sorry," I whimper. "I had to call Matt! Nick's crazy, you can't listen to him!"

Sighing again, she gets to her feet.

"Take a chill pill," she mutters, staring down at me with an expression of contempt. "It's too bad, you know. You could've shared in all the good stuff that's gonna happen. Instead, you tried to ruin it and now you're gonna get totally cut out. There's no way back for you now, Maddie. You've made your bed and now you're gonna stay in it until we decide it's safe to let you out. By then, we'll have made sure we get all the credit and all the glory for this discovery. That's Nick's plan, and he says he's got it all figured out. It's gonna suck to be you but, if it's any consolation, it's gonna be totally awesome to be me and Nick."

"Alex, please," I reply breathlessly, trying desperately to not panic, "you can't do this. You can't tie me up and leave me down here!"

"Of course I can," she says nonchalantly, before turning and making her way back over toward the steps. "See? I can do whatever the hell I like. I mean, what are you gonna do about it? As far as I can tell, your only real shot in this situation is some kinda superhero-style ability to whine and complain. You're good at looking pathetic, too. Maybe you can try to melt the ropes with those sad puppy-dog eyes of yours."

"The police are already coming," I tell her, sniffing back more tears. "They'll be here any minute!"

Stopping in the doorway, she turns and looks at me, and after a moment a faint smile crosses her lips.

"What are you going to do when they show up?" I ask breathlessly. "They'll be here in an hour, at most. Do you think you can get everything you need in an hour? And then what? Do you think you can explain it all away?"

"No," she replies calmly, "I don't think we can get everything we need in an hour, and I don't think we can explain anything away. So it's a good thing we have as long as we want." She pauses, and then her smile grows. "If you're sitting there thinking your boyfriend'll come back with the cavalry, then think again. While I've been dealing with you, Nick made sure to slow your buddy down. I'm pretty sure no-one's gonna come and interrupt us, but thanks for the concern. It's real nice to know that you're finally on our side."

"Come on!" Nick shouts from upstairs, sounding more than a little bored. "You're taking forever!"

"What did you do?" I ask, as Alex pulls the door shut, leaving me in pitch darkness down here in the basement. "Alex, what did you do? Where's Matt?"

"Watch out for ghosts!" she yells from the other side, and then I hear her hurrying up the steps.

"What did you do?" I shout. "Alex, come back! You can't leave me down here!" I pull hard on the ropes, but they feel way too firm and strong for me to slip free. Not that I stop trying, of course. "Alex!" I scream, twisting this way and that as my desperation grows. "Come back! Alex, don't do this! Where's Matt? Alex!"

I wait, but now all I hear is my own heavy breaths in the cold darkness. I can feel my heart pounding, and a moment later I hear the distant sound of footsteps somewhere else in the house.

"Alex!" I shout at the top of my voice. "Please! Don't listen to Nick! Help me!"

I start pulling on the ropes again, determined to somehow get free. I can't feel them giving at all, not even slightly, but I don't know what else I'm supposed to do. Twisting around, I press my feet against the stone column and start pushing, straining as hard as I can manage until I feel as if my ankles might be about to shatter. I keep trying, pushing and pushing as hard as possible, but I can tell that the ropes aren't budging at all and finally my feet sleep. Slumping against the cold floor, I take a moment to get my breath back as I try to figure out some other way to get free. Then I turn and start kicking the column, just in case there are any loose sections, but finally I slump back down against the cold stone floor and stare up into pitch darkness.

She'll come back.

She has to come back.

There's no way Alex would leave me down here like this. In fact, the more I think about it, the more I feel certain that she's just pulling another of her dumb pranks. Any minute now, she and Nick are going to burst through the door and admit that they've been trolling me, and then they'll laugh their asses off as they untie me. I guess I fell for yet another stupid joke, albeit one that they've taken even further than usual. Still, sitting here now in this completely dark, completely sealed basement, I'm already starting to worry that I might get short of air. Although there's a part of me that's determined to wait this out and not give Alex and Nick the satisfaction of acting like I'm panicked, I don't think I can just sit here for hours and hours until they decide to stop messing around.

In fact, I think I can even feel the air getting a little thinner now.

"Alex!" I shout, louder than before, despite the fact that my throat is starting to hurt. "It's really cold down here! Alex, can you please just let me out?"

I wait, but there's still no reply. I know they're in the house somewhere, but so far all I hear is -

Suddenly there's a bumping sound nearby. I turn and look to my left, just in time to hear a second bump that seems to be coming from way off at the far end of the basement. I can't see anything at all, but a moment later I realize that there's a very faint shuffling sound, as if something is brushing against the floor.

As if something's moving down here.

I instinctively pull back, worried that maybe Nick is hiding somewhere close. Then again, when I woke up there was still some light in here, and I'm pretty sure I'd have seen Nick if he was around. Besides, Alex said he was upstairs, and I think I even heard his voice. I guess there's a possibility that they tied Matt down here too, but again I'm sure Alex would have pointed that out.

Bumping against the stone pillar, I'm about to call out and ask if anyone's here when my bound hands brush against a set of carved grooves at the pillar's base. I run my fingertips against those grooves, and I'm shocked to find that there seem to be yet more of those strange symbols down here. Whoever put them here, he or she must have been really frantic.

And then, a moment later, I hear the sound of something metallic falling against the stone floor over on the far side of the basement.

"Hello?" I say cautiously, unable to hide the fear in my voice as I stare out into the darkness. "Is anybody here?"

CHAPTER SEVEN
DOCTOR CHARLES GRAZIER

Thursday October 4th, 1888

I take the scissors.

***

THE LAUGHTER KEEPS COMING, wave after wave, and I cannot help myself. Standing in the lavatory at Scotland Yard, I have a hand clamped across my mouth, yet still I cannot stifle my amusement at this turn of events. It is as if some great release has granted me a degree of peace for the first time in...

In how long?

Since the night Catherine first coughed up blood, perhaps?

Since Jack first showed up at my house?

Since Catherine's body rose from the slab and

began to scream?

Outside, waiting for me, is a man of Scotland Yard who truly believes that he has identified Jack the Ripper. He is absolutely serious, and he is absolutely wrong. For a moment, earlier, I worried that he had begun to suspect *me*, but now it is almost as if some great plan has managed to fool the idiot completely. There *was* no plan, of course, at least not in this regard. Yet suddenly I am presented with the possibility that this whole sorry chapter in my life can be closed, and that I can ride off into the sunset with my beloved Catherine. And that Thomas Culpepper, whose body will of course never be found, will take the blame for everything.

First, though, I must cease this endless fit of giggles. Why can I not stop laughing?

***

She struggles violently, even though the battle is lost.

***

"This one," I continue, pointing at another corpse as I walk swiftly through the room, "this one was killed by the Ripper."

I point at another.

"This one was not. That one there, that was not either."

I point at yet another.

"Nor that one."

Then I point at two more, arranged on a table at

the far end.

"Those two were not. And over here -"

"Hang on, Sir," Sanderson says, and I turn to see him making notes on a piece of paper. "I'm struggling to keep up here."

"It would be quicker," I reply, "if I were to simply tell you which of these bodies *are* the work of Jack the Ripper. After all, the vast majority of the specimens assembled in this room are nothing more than the victims of slovenly copycats."

"Are you sure, Sir?" he asks, sounding a little breathless as he makes more notes. "Perhaps you'd like to examine them a little more closely?"

"And why would I need to do that?" I reply. "Your own doctors might struggle to see the truth, but to me it is all very evident indeed."

"And you're certain?"

"I am." Reaching the end of the row, I point at two more bodies. "Those two were not killed by the Ripper."

Filled with a sense of great satisfaction, I turn to Sanderson and see that he has stopped nearby, and that he is staring at me with an expression of blank incredulity on his face. The man is clearly hanging on my every word. I know that I should have led him astray, and lied about which bodies were killed by Jack the Ripper, but I could not bring myself to ignore my very special skills. My killings were, in a way, works of art, and they should be properly acknowledged, even if the name of the artist is mis-attributed.

After a moment, I realize that Sanderson has

stopped scribbling, and that he is still staring at me.

"Well?" I ask. "What's the matter, man? Out with it."

"Well, it's just..."

He hesitates for a moment, looking around at the dead women, before turning to me again.

"There are so *few* of them," he adds.

"What do you mean?"

"I mean we have scores of dead bodies, but according to you less than a handful were killed by the real Jack the Ripper."

"Indeed," I reply, "that is the case. The rest were murdered by copycats, or simply died in the course of their everyday lives. Finding those who died at the hands of the Ripper is like searching for diamonds in the mud. They are there, but one needs to look carefully. One must have an expert eye for these things."

"We have never had a killer like this before," he explains, still seeming more than a little baffled. "Not somebody who carried out such a sustained campaign of murder."

"Of course you have," I say with a sigh. "It is merely that this is the first time that you have noticed."

"How do you mean, Doctor Grazier?"

"The streets of London are filled with killers," I remind him. "Why, I am sure there must be murders every night, especially in the lowly areas around the docks. But do you investigate those murders fully, Inspector Sanderson?"

"Some are put down to brawls and drunken fights," he admits, a little reticently.

"Precisely," I continue. "There are so many murders, one scarcely knows where to begin sorting through them all. But this Jack the Ripper fellow has focused your attention, has he not? He has made you take the whole thing far more seriously."

"I suppose the letters made us sit up and take notice," he replies.

"The letters?"

"The letters taunting the police. Most of them are fakes, of course, but we think a couple are from the real killer. On account of information that only he'd know."

I feel a shudder pass through my chest as I recall Jack's eagerness to pen missive after missive to the investigators. In truth, I rather distracted him from that purpose, but it was the letters that excited his interest when he first came to my home.

"I cannot help you there," I tell Sanderson. "I would not put too much stock in the letters, if I were you."

"But they tell us something about the killer," he explains. "The ones that were really from him, I mean. Some of them went into great detail about specific things that only the murderer could have known." He sighs. "He must be a madman. Skilled, yes, and educated, but utterly, utterly insane. Some of the fellows here think that we can analyze the handwriting and the structure of the sentences, that sort of thing, and get to understand the killer's mind a little better."

"Understand his mind?" I reply, furrowing my brow. "Whatever can that mean?"

"There are some new theories coming in from the rest of Europe," he continues. "Apparently you can tell a lot about a man if you study his mind. There's a word for it, psycho-something. Doesn't make much sense to me, but smarter folk round these parts reckon it might be useful. I think the idea is that people give stuff away about themselves, Sir, without intending to. They sort of let things slip through body language."

"The whole thing sounds like poppycock," I say with a sigh. "You can tell a great deal about a man from what he says, and from how he comports himself, but there are limits."

"But the depths of the mind -"

"The human mind is by its very nature a shallow thing," I add, interrupting him. "A man says something, and he does something, and that is the end of the matter. If one tries to go rooting around in other aspects, one will surely end up wasting one's time. And that, Inspector Sanderson, is advice that you would do well to take and consider."

"Tell me, Doctor Grazier... Did you ever see any sign that Doctor Culpepper could be so deranged?"

"I did not," I reply, and I have to stifle a smile as I think back to Culpepper's quiet, sedate manner. "He showed no hint of it at all. Indeed, the man appeared to be utterly devoid of any particularly strong characteristic. In any direction."

"He never mentioned murdering people, or anything like that?"

I can scarcely stifle a laugh. "No, Inspector Sanderson," I manage to say finally, "he did not. That sort of talk, I'd wager, would most certainly have caught my attention. Truly, Doctor Thomas Culpepper was a weak and feeble fellow, the type who'd barely say boo to a goose."

"He was the most heinous killer in England's history," Sanderson says darkly, "and I find it difficult to imagine that he shall ever be surpassed."

"Then you, Sir," I reply, "should study human nature in a little more depth. Because no matter what you think of this Ripper, I can assure you that there will always be worse people out there, conducting their work in private, until the whole of human civilization comes crashing to the ground. In that regard, Jack the Ripper is surely just the tip of a very nasty iceberg."

CHAPTER EIGHT
MADDIE

Today

I DON'T KNOW HOW LONG I've spent sitting in complete silence, staring into the darkness, but it must be at least ten minutes. And so far, there have been no more sounds.

Behind my back, my fingertips are still touching the symbols that I've found carved into the stone pillar. I've managed to make out a square so far, and some kind of triangle, and various lines that don't seem to form any particular shape. Still, I've felt just enough to be sure these are like the symbols I found in other parts of the house. I still don't have any idea what they mean, but it's become increasingly clear that someone was obsessed with carving them all around the place. Doctor Charles Grazier, perhaps? Or was he really so superstitious? Maybe there was somebody else here in the house with him.

It's also becoming clear that Alex and Nick aren't coming down to reveal their prank any time soon. In fact, I'm starting to worry that for once they're being serious. Either that, or they've forgotten me.

I've already given up trying to get the ropes loose. They're tied way too tight, and every time I try to pull one wrist loose, I only end up making the other worse. I've also given up trying to shout for help, because I'm sure nobody would be able to hear me from all the way down here. My only hope right now – sitting in darkness and not even able to see my own knees thanks to the complete absence of any light – is that Matt's going to come back soon with reinforcements. I don't want to rely on him, but he's the only chance I've got. Matt's smart. Matt wouldn't let himself get tricked by Alex and Nick. Matt knows what he's doing.

And then there's the rustling sound.

For the past few minutes, a very subtle rustling sound has begun to pick up, out there in the darkness. I think it's coming from somewhere to my left, far off by the wall near the counters, but it's difficult to be certain. What I *can* tell is that something seems to be persistently moving about, or maybe the sound is more like a constant low whisper. I keep telling myself that there's probably just a rat down here – not that a rat makes me feel any better – but the sound is starting to make the hairs on the back of my neck stand up.

There's no such thing as ghosts, I tell myself.

Somehow, though, those words no longer feel quite so reassuring.

A few minutes later, however, the sound fades away.

I don't have a clue how I'm going to get out of here, but one thing's certain: I can't just sit here like a complete idiot, waiting for someone to come and untie me. I start pulling on the ropes again, even though the whole situation feels completely hopeless and despite the chafing burns that are already developing around my wrists. I've tried telling myself that there has to be a way out of here, that there's no such thing as an impossible situation, but I can't quite get myself to believe any of that just yet. If there *is* a way out, maybe I'm just too dumb to figure it out.

And then, suddenly, the whispering sound returns, this time just behind my right shoulder and much, much closer.

"He was a good man," a voice says. "Such a good man."

I freeze, certain that I actually heard those words. A moment later I hear the rustling sound again, before the voice returns behind my left shoulder.

"He was the best man, but he became obsessed. He thought he could defeat death itself."

I turn and look into the darkness, and now my heart is pounding.

"Who's there?" I ask, and I can hear the fear in my own voice. I'm starting to shiver, too, as the temperature seems to plummet all around me. "Who are you?"

I wait, but now there's only silence.

"Alex, is that you?" I continue, although I

already know the answer. Alex definitely left the basement, and besides the voice sounded nothing like her. It was older somehow, although definitely female, and it sounded like someone pretty posh. Still, it's the only explanation.

"Alex, this isn't funny!" I hiss, letting my anger through into my voice. "Let me out of here right now!"

I wait a moment longer, and then I turn the other way, staring out into the darkness.

"Alex!" I shout. "You're being -"

"He didn't mean to hurt them," the voice says suddenly, coming from directly in front of me.

"Who are you?" I yell, pulling back against the pillar. I'm trembling more and more, and I swear the temperature is still dropping. "What do you want?"

"He wasn't thinking properly," the voice continues, sounding a little quieter now but also a little more sorrowful, almost as if the person is about to burst into tears. "I told him not to let it change him, but he couldn't stop. He couldn't accept defeat. He let the desperation and the bitterness seep into his heart, and then it froze and cracked his goodness."

"Who are you?" I ask again. "What are you talking about? I can't see you."

"He believed he could do anything," the voice says, suddenly coming closer again. At the same time, the air in front of me becomes even colder. I'm shivering so badly, my teeth are starting to chatter. "He let it drive him mad. I tried to stop him but he wouldn't listen, not even after it was too late. And then at the end, what he did to that poor baby..."

I wait, too scared to move an inch.

Finally I open my mouth to ask "Who are you?" again, but at the last moment I stop myself as I realize that I need to try a different approach. Yelling and crying out hasn't helped at all, and I haven't been able to escape, so there's only one other possibility.

"My name's Maddie," I say cautiously. "Maddie Harper. Can you help me get out of here? I'll do anything you want, anything I *can* do, but can you please help me?"

I wait, and now the cold air seems to move slightly, as if somebody is so close that I could almost touch them.

"Such a good man," the voice whispers softly, sounding closer but also weaker. "He never would have done that to the woman and her baby, not unless he'd lost his mind. You have to believe me. And now he won't speak to me. He knows what he did, and he hides in the shadows. He won't even show his face, and I love him so much. Despite everything he did, he's still my Charles..."

The voice fades, and slowly the temperature starts creeping back up to normal.

"Who are you?" I ask for what must be the fifth or sixth time. I look around, but still all I see is absolute pitch darkness. "Come back! Whoever you are, I need to talk to you! I need your help!"

The only answer, however, is silence.

"Can you call someone?" I continue, with tears in my eyes again. "If you can't untie me, can you go and get help?"

I start pulling on the ropes again, but my wrists

are still bound far too tight. I'm starting to feel a stronger sense of panic and – although I keep telling reminding myself that there's no such thing as ghosts – I can't help thinking that the voice didn't belong to anyone who's supposed to be in this house. I even try to persuade myself that I imagined the whole thing, that somehow I've begun to experience aural hallucinations, but I can't quite get that idea to stick. Instead, I start frantically pulling at the ropes, ignoring the pain in my wrists as I tug harder and harder, trying everything I can think of to get myself loose. Finally, as I start to feel beads of blood running down from my wrists and onto the palms of my hand, I let out a sigh as I lean back against the pillar and try to think of another idea.

I have to get out of here.

I don't care what it takes, but I have to find a way.

At the same time, I have no idea what I'm supposed to try next. Tears are welling in my eyes, and I'm starting to worry that Alex and Nick might just leave me down here. What if they take everything they need from the house and just let me starve to death? Then again, they'll need to be able to show people into the place, so I guess they can't just let me rot down here, in which case...

Suddenly I realize that they might be planning something worse, and for a moment the absolute worst case scenario floods into my mind. What if they kill me, to get me out of the way? I try to tell myself that they're not that crazy, but the truth is that I don't really know anything about Nick at all, and I'm worried that he seems to have a lot of influence over Alex. And while I don't want to believe that Alex would get involved with anything truly awful, I can't help thinking back to something she said before she left the basement:

"If you're sitting there thinking your boyfriend'll come back with the cavalry, then think again. While I've been dealing with you, Nick made sure to slow your buddy down."

What exactly does that mean?

What have they done to Matt?

What -

"What can we do?" a man's voice asks suddenly, somewhere nearby in the darkness. "Can we sedate her?"

I freeze, listening to the silence that has fallen now. I want to believe that the voice was another hallucination, but deep down I already know that it was real. My heart is pounding, and I know that the voice didn't come from Nick. It was too deep, too full, just different in every way.

And then, suddenly, it returns:

"Perhaps we should screw her mouth shut. Or wrap wire around her jaw."

CHAPTER NINE
DOCTOR CHARLES GRAZIER

Thursday October 4th, 1888

I cut.

***

BELLS RING OUT FROM A NEARBY CHURCH as I make my way along the street. Whereas usually I find London to be rather overcrowded, this afternoon I am actually enjoying a perambulation through the fair city. Indeed, for the first time in my life I feel almost as if I am one of Monseiur Baudelaire's people, a flaneur, enjoying the serious work of walking along street after street. Perhaps some inner comfort has afforded me this opportunity.

After leaving Scotland Yard, I make my way along Whitehall and through Trafalgar Square, then up through Soho and further to Fitzrovia. It was not my intention, upon leaving the police offices, to walk for such a long distance, but I find myself lost in thought and unable to even contemplate summoning a ride home. I surprise myself a few minutes later, when I actually stop and go into the Langham, where I spend an hour enjoying the most exquisite afternoon tea. This is not something I would usually do, but somehow I feel today as if I want to be around people. I sit listening to the conversations of everyone around me, although many of them are gossiping about the latest murders. Still, the tea is excellent, and when I finally leave I do something that would usually horrify me: I leave a gratuity for the waiter, as a reward for his fine service.

Once I am underway again, Fitzrovia gives way to Regent's Park, by which point I realize that I am rather straying from the route home. I deviate west and pass by the British Library on my way through to Clerkenwell. I am now not too distant from home, so I take a detour past the market at Spitalfields before noticing that my legs are becoming rather tired. I am an older man, physically, even if my mind remains youthful.

And then, stopping near Brick Lane, I suddenly realize that I can hear a whispering voice behind me. I walk on a few paces, determined to shake the fellow off, but the whispering continues and finally I have no choice but to turn and address whoever seems to be dogging my tracks.

Except that there is nobody to be seen.

I look around, but I am quite alone here on the street. Unnerved but determined to enjoy my walk some more, I set off in the direction of Vallance Road. Night is beginning to fall, and in my role as a flaneur I cannot help but note the change in the streets as those who work by day give way to those who work by night. Perhaps once all of this fuss is over, I shall dedicate my remaining years to the task of writing a biography of these streets. While some men strive furiously to write books about people of note, I shall write a book about the streets of London. Each shall be given its own section, and I shall attempt to draw out the individual character of each. Catherine can assist me, and -

Suddenly hearing the whisper again, I turn and look back the way I have come.

There is still no sign of anyone, other than a few passersby who pay me no attention, but then a moment later I spot a woman watching me from the shadowed alley that runs down the side of a butcher's shop. Whoever she is, this woman has her eyes fixed on me completely, and there is something about her stare that makes me feel rather unsettled. Her eyes seem very dark and perhaps even sunken, and her color is distinctly pale. Indeed, I lower my spectacles for a moment, just to be sure that the tinted glass is not deceiving me, and now I see that the woman is indeed somehow set apart from her surroundings. A gentle breeze is blowing along the street, but this woman's dress seems entirely untroubled.

And still she watches me.

A moment later, I realize that the air seems to be becoming rather cold.

Turning, I resolve to set off and give the matter no further thought. No sooner am I at the end of the next street, however, than I hear another, rather different type of whisper coming from nearby. I glance in the direction, and I am startled to see another girl watching me from behind the window of a rather unkempt-looking house. She is barely visible in the gloom, but I can just make out her bare, featureless expression staring at me from the other side of a mottled glass pane. There can be no doubt that I am the object of this wretched creature's attention, and I am stopped in my tracks as I wait in vain for her to look elsewhere.

"Stop that!" I call out to her finally. "Go away! Leave me alone!"

Yet still she stares, still she seems to carve into my mind with her gaze. I raise my cane and use it to tap the window, but this does nothing to deter her.

"Absurd thing," I mutter, turning and walking away. "The mad should be locked up, not left to bother decent people."

When I reach the next corner, however, I hear another whisper, and then another. I turn and look over my shoulder, and I find that two more girls have appeared, and that they seem to be following me along the street. Now that I am stopped, they stop too, just a few feet away, but they stare at me with a strange intensity that I cannot deny leaves me feeling rather troubled. They are making no secret of the fact that I am the object of their attention, and they seem – though clearly poor and destitute – to think that they have all the right in the world to be troubling me in this manner. Whatever is the world coming to?

"What do you want?" I snap. "Go on, away with

you!"

I wait, but they do not respond. After a moment, however, I notice a dark stain beginning to show itself on the front of the dress worn by one of the girls. It is almost as if blood itself is starting to soak through, although I know that this is not possible. I am about to tell the girl that she must attend to herself, when I suddenly realize that something about her countenance and face strikes me as being a little familiar. Obviously I could never have come into contact with such a creature before, however, so I simply turn and hurry on.

And the whispers follow.

At first I do not look back. I refuse to pay any attention to such trivial things, yet the whispers persist and perhaps even begin to grow in strength. Indeed, by the time I get to the next street corner I feel as if these infernal voices are poised to slip into my ears and penetrate my thoughts directly. I should continue to ignore them, of course, but instead I stop and turn, and I am shocked to see that now there are half a dozen of these pale, lifeless faces staring at me.

"Leave me alone!" I shout, waving my hand at them. "Whatever you want, you shan't get it from me! Now go away before there's trouble!"

"Are you alright, Sir?" a man asks, stopping nearby. "Do you require assistance?"

"Of course not," I stammer. "I just wish to be rid of these horrific things! They've been following me for several streets now and I'm beginning to tire of their foolish antics."

He turns and looks toward the girls, although he

seems neither surprised nor shocked by the sight of them. Indeed, after a moment he turns and furrows his brow as he regards me.

"It is not right," I continue, "that a gentleman should be pursued through the streets in such a manner." I turn to the girls. "If you do not leave me alone at once, I shall have no option but to find a police officer and speak to him! Then you'll be in trouble, won't you?!?"

"Please do!" one of the girls says suddenly, stepping toward me. "Fetch the police. We should like to speak to them as well."

"What are you talking about?" I ask, before turning to the nearby gentleman and seeing that he seems quite shocked, although his gaze is fixed upon me rather than upon these awful girls. "Do you see what I meant? I am being harassed! In public!"

"Perhaps you should wait right here," he replies, and now a couple of other men have stopped as well. "I shall go and find somebody who can help you. Don't worry, they'll take good care of you, but I think you could use a little aid."

"All I need is for these ghouls to leave me alone!" I roar. "What else am I supposed to do, when I am followed through the streets in such a manner? Why, this kind of treatment is intolerable. I've got half a mind to take my cane and whack them all around their heads, just to beat some sense into them!"

"Followed?" one of the other men mutters, before turning to his companion. "Is the man quite deranged?"

"Don't you see them?" I shout, gesturing toward

the pale girls. "What's wrong with you? What -"

Suddenly my spectacles slip from my nose. I try to catch them, but they merely land in the palm of my hand. I quickly re-arrange them in their proper place, but when I glance at the gentlemen I see that they are staring at me with expressions of the utmost horror.

"What in the name of all that's holy is wrong with this fellow?" one of them asks.

"His eyes," another man whispers, "they looked..."

"Are we going to the police now?" one of the pale girls adds, stepping closer and chilling the air around me as she does so. "There is so much we should like to tell them about you, Sir. We have tried, but they don't hear us. Nobody hears us, except you."

"Intolerable," I mutter, taking a step back. "Utterly intolerable. Whatever is going on in this once-proud city?"

"Yes," one of the other girls says, her voice barely rising above a whisper. "What *has* London come to, that monsters roam the streets?"

"Come and sit down," one of the men says, reaching out toward me. "You seem to be in rather a bad way, Sir, and we can send for medical help. I'm sure there's nothing seriously wrong, but it'd be a good idea to get checked out."

"Yes, sit down," one of the girls says, once again chilling the air as she comes closer. "More of us are coming. The dead of London are gathering, Sir. Sit right here and wait for us."

"No!" I shout, pushing them all away and

rushing along the street. "Never!"

"Sir, come back!" a man shouts. "Sir, you're not well! Let us help you!"

CHAPTER TEN
MADDIE

Today

SITTING IN ABJECT, TERRIFIED SILENCE, I listen as a voice continues to whisper in the darkness. Most of the time, the voice is too soft and too quiet for me to make out what it's saying, but occasionally it seems to become a little stronger and clearer, and I can pick out snatches of sentences. Sure enough, a moment later I manage to hear a few words:

"I can still feel her trying to open her mouth, Sir. If I let go, even slightly..."

And then it's too quiet again, although I can still hear the faintest whisper. And at the same time, I've begun to notice that every time the words become clear, I experience the taste of peaches in my mouth. I lick my lips, convinced that the taste has to be some kind of illusion, but if anything it seemed to be getting even stronger.

"Who are you?" I whisper, pressing myself back against the stone pillar. "Please, who -"

Suddenly I hear a loud bumping sound, as if something metal just dropped against the floor. I turn and look into the darkness, and almost immediately I hear the sound of footsteps coming closer. I flinch, but the footsteps move past me and head toward the darkness at the far end of the basement. The air all around is getting colder, and there's no doubt now that somebody is down here with me. And although the taste of peaches seemed strong a moment ago, now it's almost overpowering.

"Please let me go," I stammer as the low whisper continues, and as tears run down my face. "Please, whoever you are, you have to let me go."

"What of the kidneys and the liver?" the voice asks suddenly.

"What?" I reply.

All I hear now, however, is more faint whispers. Whoever's down here, they seem to be completely ignoring me, but they're also not trying to hide their presence. I don't understand how they can be working in the dark, but I guess maybe they have some kind of night-vision system. I can hear occasional bumps and footsteps, as if they're getting on with some kind of task.

"Please," I whisper, "you have to let me go, I only -"

"Doctor Grazier," the voice says suddenly, sounding a little fearful, "I -"

And then it's gone, this time sounding as if it

was cut off in mid-sentence. I hear footsteps again, and I pull away as they seem to march straight past me. Then I hear a bumping sound coming from straight ahead, I think from somewhere near the slab in the middle of the room. The sound returns a couple more times, accompanied by a faint rattling, and then I hear a tired, heavy gasp.

Then silence.

Absolute, yawning silence, without even a whisper.

"Please," I say after a moment, "I don't know who you are or why you're doing this, but -"

Suddenly the room is filled with an ear-splitting scream. I instinctively reach up and try to put my hands over my ears, but the ropes are just a little too short and all I can do instead is listen as the scream gets louder and louder. If anything, however, the scream seems almost to be coming from somewhere inside my head, shaking my skull so much that a pulsing pain runs across my forehead. And then, with no warning, the scream ends as abruptly as it began, and I hear a shuffling sound nearby.

"As I warned you," the voice says, "there has been no change. Sir -"

And that's where it stops, seemingly cut off in mid-sentence.

Suddenly the scream returns, sounding even louder than before. This time I start pulling away, shuffling around the stone pillar in what I already know is a futile attempt to get away. The ropes allow me to get all the way around to the pillar's other side, but the scream seems to be ringing out through my skull, and finally I let out a scream of my own. As soon as I do so, however, the sound stops. I cry out for a moment longer before managing to fall silent.

"I assure you, Doctor Grazier," the voice says seconds later, "I did what I was told, and nothing more or less. I have learned from the mistakes I made in the past. I cannot claim to know what is wrong with your wife, but I am absolutely sure that it is not of my doing."

Doctor Grazier?

Why is the voice saying that name? Doctor Charles Grazier has been dead for more than a century.

"Are you sure that it *is* your wife, Sir?" the voice adds suddenly. "She does not seem human, Sir. I am sorry."

I hear more whispers, but they seem a lot fainter now, as if they're fading away. I don't dare call out this time, so instead I simply sit in the darkness and wait as the basement falls silent. I'm convinced that the man's voice will return at any moment, and I'm shaking with fear. In the back of my mind, I'm already starting to think that somehow I heart ghosts, but I keep telling myself over and over that there's no such things.

I refuse to believe that I heard the voices of dead people.

They were just hallucinations, like all the other things I saw while I was on the streets. Clearly there's something wrong with me, something that makes me imagine crazy scenarios whenever I'm scared or stressed. That's got to be a pretty major flaw in my character, and I'm going to have to figure it out later, but right now I have to stay focused. Despite the tears that are streaming down my face, I tell myself to stay calm and focus on getting out of here. If I let my fears take over, I'm going to end up losing my mind and dying down here. At the same time, I can't help replaying those voices over and over in my mind, and I'm not sure I'm strong enough to keep them out.

"Please," I whisper, squeezing my eyes tight shut even though I'm already in darkness. "Keep it together, Maddie. Don't lose your mind, don't -"

Suddenly the peach taste bursts into my mouth, and this time I let out a chocking gasp as I feel hundreds of tiny, sharp edges rushing up from the back of my throat. Unable to breathe, I try to pull away from the pillar, but now there are even more of these hard little legs scurrying into my mouth, and I can feel bugs or beetles swarming out onto my face. I try to spit them away, but my throat is swelling as more and more of them rise up through my body, and finally I bite down hard, hoping to kill them so that I can try to get a breath of air.

I lean forward, spewing the corpses out, but there are fresh live bugs already crawling up into the back of my mouth. At the same time, the taste of peaches is somehow becoming even stronger, and I can feel my eyes starting to bulge as I begin to suffocate.

And then they're gone.

Suddenly all the bugs vanish, and the peach taste goes away.

"He was a good man," the female voice whispers suddenly.

Startled, I let out a cry as I pull away. The ropes

hold tight, keeping my against the stone pillar, but I'm shaking violently now and I can feel myself giving in to the madness. I'm struggling to get my breath back, and I'm terrified that the bugs are going to come back at any moment. I know they weren't real, that they *can't* have been real, but at the same time I'm frantically scared that I might feel them again. I want to be strong, and to hold my mind together, but the voices are just too clear and too powerful. I know that I have to push the voices away, and that I have to get out of here before the bugs come back.

"He was the greatest man I ever met," the female voice says. "He was -"

"Go away!" I scream, pulling harder than ever against the ropes. "Leave me alone! Get out of my head!"

"He was so proud and so good," the voice continues, as if it didn't hear me at all. "He was just led astray, that's all. He wouldn't let me go. People mustn't think that he was a monster. I loved him, and he was no monster. He was my husband."

"GET OUT OF MY HEAD!" I shout again, before breaking down into a series of heavy, shuddering sobs. "Get out of my head," I whimper through the tears as I start rocking back and forth as much as the ropes will allow. "Get out of my head, get out of my head, get out of my head..."

"It was love that made him do what he did," the voice whispers. "Love for me. I would do anything to get him back. Anything. When he killed the child, his mind shattered."

"Leave me alone," I sob through gritted teeth, still shaking all over. "Go away!"

I'm crying so much, it actually takes several minutes before I notice that the voice has finally stopped. I open my eyes in the darkness and sit listening to the silence all around. Terrified that the voice is going to come back at any moment, or that I'll feel the bugs again, I don't dare believe that I might have actually pushed the madness away. I keep telling myself that the voices were *only* voices, that they can't actually hurt me, and that the bugs were all in my imagination. If I can hold onto that simple fact, maybe I can pull myself together.

Suddenly I hear a scraping sound over on the far side of the basement. I turn and look into the darkness, and a moment later there's a metal bumping sound. I wait, too scared to even call out, as the scraping sound returns and starts moving this way. Something's coming across the floor, making its way straight toward me. I try to pull back, but I can't really maneuver properly and tears are streaming down my face as I hear the sound getting closer and closer. If it's another bug, or a swarm of them, I think my heart might give out.

"Please don't hurt me," I whimper, finally unable to keep from panicking. "Please, leave me alone."

The scraping sound continues.

"It's just a noise," I say out loud, hoping to regain control of my senses. "It can't hurt you. It's just a noise, it can't do anything to you."

I start kicking frantically, desperate to get the

bugs away.

"It's just a noise!" I scream. "It's just -"

Before I can finish, something bumps against my hand. I let out a loud shriek and pull away, but then the scraping sound returns and my hand is hit again. This time, however, I feel what seems to be something small and solid. I hesitate for a moment, still terrified, before finally reaching through the darkness until my fingers brush against the object. I wait a moment, in case anything else happens, and then I start feeling the rest of the shape as I slowly realize what I've found.

It's a knife.

One of the knives from the counter has somehow ended up over here, and a moment later my fingertips brush against the serrated blade.

I hesitate for a moment longer, before grabbing the knife and furiously starting to cut through the ropes.

CHAPTER ELEVEN
DOCTOR CHARLES GRAZIER

Thursday October 4th, 1888

I take a knife from the side and step around the slab, before reaching down and cutting Delilah's throat as she continues to wriggle and squirm.

***

"NO MORE!" I shout, pressing my back against the front door, causing it to slam shut. "No more," I gasp, "please, no more..."

Slithering down to the floor, I feel a shudder pass through my chest.

"No more," I say again, "no more, no more..."

I wait, hearing only the sound of my own breathlessness. After a moment, however, I realize I can hear the whispers once again, coming from outside.

Getting to my feet, I slide the bolt across the door and hurry to the window, and when I look outside I see scores of those pale dead girls coming along the street. It is as if I drew more and more of them to my side as I rushed home, but I am certain they shall not bother me now, not in my own home. They cannot get in here. An Englishman's home is his castle and I refuse to let those *things* through my door.

"What madness is this?" I whisper, taking a step back. "What -"

Suddenly I hear the most tremendous banging sound, strong enough to make the floorboards shudder beneath me. I look down, lost in confusion and panic, and it takes fully a few seconds before I remember what I left in the basement before heading out this morning. I was hoping to come home and find that Catherine would have recovered her proper mind, yet the continued banging seems to indicate that the beastly creature retains control of her body. Still, I am certain that success will come soon. I must simply stay strong.

***

Blood sprays from her gashed neck. I have to stand back to avoid getting splattered. Her body is shaking violently.

***

"Catherine?" I whisper, standing in the basement and staring at the door that leads into the storage area. "Can you hear me?"

I wait in silence, but I hear no reply. She is behind that door, where she has remained ever since I locked her inside a few days ago. It has been more than twenty-four hours since I forced the vile, pinkish liquid through the gap at the bottom of the door, and I know I heard her licking it all up. That means that the concoction entered her body, which in turn means that it must surely by now have finished coursing through her veins. Any moment now, that infusion of youth and new life will surely begin to take effect.

Any moment.

Perhaps even *this* moment.

"Catherine?" I say again, raising my voice a little. "Do you hear me? It is I, your husband, your darling Charles. I have worked so long and so hard to rectify the nightmare that broke out in our lives. I know you can hear me, so listen to my voice and allow me to guide you back to the light."

Again I wait.

Again I hear nothing.

My first instinct is to turn around and go back upstairs, to wait perhaps until tomorrow morning, yet instead I walk toward the door and reach out to touch its wooden surface. Since the banging sound that followed my return to the house, I have neither seen nor heard any further indication that Catherine is still moving around, yet I know that she must be there. Perhaps this period of silence is a good sign, perhaps it means that her true mind is reasserting control over that *thing* that took control of her body.

"Catherine," I whisper, "I know you can hear me. Say something. Say anything."

I keep my hand pressed against the cold wood, and I try to imagine her in the same position on the other side. Waking, finally, back into her body.

"I shall return shortly," I tell her finally, moving my hand away. "I shall not give up on you, my dear. While there is still breath and blood in my body, I shall work tirelessly to get you back."

I hesitate for a moment longer, just to give her a chance to speak, and then I turn and start walking back toward the stairs.

"Release me," a gasping voice says suddenly, causing me to stop in my tracks.

My heart is beating so fast, I swear I can feel it pounding in my chest, and a cold sweat has in an instant broken across my face. I know that I heard her, but I cannot bring myself to believe that she is finally speaking.

"Release me from here," the voice says again, coming from behind the door. "It's so dark and cold in here. Open this thing and let me out."

I turn slowly, but all I see is the still-closed door.

"Release me now," the voice continues, and I hear a faint scratching sound coming from the door's other side. "I am hungry again, and so thirsty."

My heart soars.

"Catherine?" I whisper. "Catherine, is that you?"

"Who is Catherine?" the voice replies.

"What -"

Stopping myself, I realize that all hope is once

again lost.

"Who is Catherine?" she asks again.

"Catherine is my wife," I stammer, trying to stay calm even though I can feel my body beginning to tremble all over with fear. "Catherine, is that you? Your voice... I cannot tell."

I wait, but there is no reply.

"Catherine," I continue, stepping closer to the door. "For the love of -"

"Yes," the voice says suddenly, accompanied by more scratching sounds. "Catherine. That is my name. I am Catherine and I would like very much to be released from this place. Won't you open the door?"

"Catherine," I whisper, reaching for the bolt but then hesitating for a moment, "is it really you?"

"Of course it's really me," she replies softly. "I am Catherine, and I am so cold in here. Please, you cannot leave me to rot in this darkness for a moment longer. I have waited and waited, and this is my last chance. I am begging you, release me immediately."

"How do I know that you are real?" I ask, my voice trembling with fear.

"How do I know that *you* are real?" she replies.

I hesitate, before reaching down and sliding the bolt across. My hands are shaking violently, but somehow I manage to take the key from my pocket, although it takes several tries before I am able to get the cursed thing into the lock.

And then I pause, as I realize that there is still one more thing that I must ask.

"What is my name?"

"You can tell me your name later," she replies.

"But you should know it."

"My name is Catherine."

"And what is *my* name?"

"I'm sure it is a lovely name," she says softly, her voice almost purring. She sounds, in truth, nothing whatsoever like my dear Catherine. "I'll reward you for letting me out of here," she continues. "I'll give you anything you want, but first you must release me. Do you understand? I refuse to stay in here for a moment longer. Now that I have learned how to control this body, you will help me to find my place in the world. So much must have changed, and I am hungry to see it all. First, though, you must help me. I am so weak."

"I shall let you out," I reply, "just as soon as you tell me my name."

I wait, with tears streaming down my face, but she says nothing.

"Catherine," I continue, "if -"

"LET ME OUT!" she screams, suddenly slamming against the door from the other side.

Falling back, I slam down hard against the cold stone floor. The door rattles violently in its frame, but the key remains unturned in the lock. Still she tries to break through, and I am not entirely certain that the hinges will hold, although I am least fairly certain that it would take her quite some time to smash her way out of the room. Getting back to my feet, I force myself to step closer and slide the bolt back into its proper place.

Locked.

"LET ME OUT THIS INSTANT!" she gurgles,

her voice filled with fury. Hatred, even. "I WILL DESTROY YOU IF YOU DON'T!"

Too shocked to know how to react, I step back as she continues to smash the door, but then a moment later she stops and the basement falls silent once more.

"Please let me out," she whimpers. "I'm so cold in here. I thought you loved me? Why are you leaving me to suffer like this?"

"You are not Catherine," I reply, backing away until I reach the bottom of the steps. "My Catherine would never speak in such a manner."

"I think I shall freeze to death," she continues, and now it sounds as if she is on the verge of truly sobbing. "Why have you left me in here like this, naked and cold? Do you hate me?"

"You are not Catherine," I whisper again. "You are -"

"LET ME OUT!" she screams, suddenly slamming against the door once again. "LET ME OUT, OR I'LL FIND SOME OTHER WAY AND THEN I'LL END YOUR MISERABLE EXISTENCE!"

That is not Catherine. Everything I have done, everything I have tried, has been an utter failure. Panicking, I turn to go up the stairs.

"Charles!" she calls out suddenly. "Charles, it's me!"

I freeze.

Did she just -

"Charles, help me," she sobs, and now – finally – she sounds like Catherine. "Charles, I don't know what's happening, but I'm scared. I'm cold and I'm weak and I'm starving. Charles, why am I in here? Why have you locked me in the dark?"

I turn and look back toward the door.

"Charles, help me," she continues. "For the love of God, help me. And if you can't help me, then kill me. Just don't leave me here like this, I'm begging you to let me out!"

"Catherine?" I whisper, momentarily too shocked to move. Finally, however, I realize that something must have changed. I do not understand, but somehow she has found her way back to me after all this time.

Filled with a sudden burst of hope, I stumble across the room and quickly get to work unlocking the door.

"I am going to release you," I stammer. "Wait one moment, my dear, and you shall soon be free."

"Hurry!" she gasps. "I'm so cold, Charles. I think I might freeze to death!"

"Never!"

I pull the bolt aside and turn the key in the lock, and then I swing the door open. I expect Catherine to fall against me, but to my surprise I see that she is instead slumped against the far wall, as if she has no strength left at all. My first reaction, upon seeing the rotten flesh that still hung to her bones, is one of absolute revulsion, and I am very nearly minded to slam the door back shut. Some deeper aspect stirs in my soul, however, and finally I see her fearful, plaintive face, and I feel one absolute and very clear certainty blossom in my heart.

"Catherine!" I gasp stepping forward before

breaking into a short run and hurrying over, quickly kneeling next to her. "My darling, is it you? Are you really returned to me?"

"Charles," she whispers, her voice sounding so very frail and old. "Charles, Charles..."

"Is it really, *really* you?" I ask, but I do not wait for an answer.

Instead, I reach out and place a hand on the side of her face. Even though her flesh is tattered and torn, and rotten in some places, I feel an outpouring of absolute love as I realize that after long last, after everything that has happened, I have her back.

"Oh Catherine," I sob, leaning closer and kissing her forehead. "It was worth it. It was all worth it."

"Charles," she replies, sounding so very tired, "oh Charles... Charles Grazier... Are all men this easy to trick, or are you an exception?"

I freeze, convinced that I must have misheard, but then I pull back slightly and look into her eyes. To my horror, I see a moment later that a smile is slowly spreading across her thin, rotten lips.

"Catherine -"

Before I can finish, she lunges at me, cackling maniacally as she presses me down against the cold concrete. Landing on top of me, she sneers into my face, spraying my features with a fine layer of spittle as her bony fingers start tearing at my shirt. I try to push her away, but she is too strong and all I can do is cry out in agony as I feel her fingernails slicing down through my chest, cutting me open and causing blood to erupt from the wounds.

DOCTOR CHARLES GRAZIER

And still I scream.

CHAPTER TWELVE
MADDIE

Today

THE HANDLE CLICKS SLIGHTLY, causing me to hesitate for a moment, but then I slowly start pulling the door open so that I can see up the stairs toward the hallway.

So far, I can't hear Alex and Nick at all, but I'm certain they must still be in the house somewhere. After all, this place is supposed to be their ticket off the streets, so I doubt they'd risk leaving it alone for even a second. I take care to open the door very slowly, to minimize the risk of the hinges creaking, and then I glance over my shoulder and take a look back down into the basement.

There's still not a great deal of light, but I definitely don't see any sign that anybody else is down here with me. I watch the shadows for a moment, just in case I spot a hint of movement, but then I remind myself that my priority has to be getting out of here. Whatever else happens, whatever I might find out about this house, I have to get help.

Turning, I look up the stairs and wait a moment longer, and then I carefully step through and start making my way up into the main part of the house. After a few seconds, I realize that I've inadvertently been holding my breath. And with each step, I feel the knot of fear twisting tighter and tighter in my chest.

***

The house is completely silent.

Standing in the hallway, still holding the knife that I used to cut through the ropes, I listen for even the slightest hint that Alex and Nick are nearby. I expected to at least hear their voices in the distance, but so far it's almost as if they've left. I know that can't be the case, of course, and I'm worried that they could suddenly come at me from any of the rooms. Or, worse, that they somehow know I've escaped, and that they're waiting to ambush me at any moment.

There's a part of me that wants to go up the main staircase and search for Matt, but I quickly tell myself that I need to be smarter. The best option is to get out of here and go to Jerry's house, and call the police from there. They'll be here in five or ten minutes, and then they can grab Alex and Nick. I feel as if I'd be betraying Matt if I left, but at the same time I know that calling for help is our only chance. So as much as I feel an urge to start playing the role of amateur superhero, I start carefully edging toward the open back door so that -

Suddenly I freeze as I hear them.

Alex and Nick are in the back garden. I peer out, and then I immediately pull back as I see that they're sitting on the grass just a few meters from the door, smoking cigarettes. There's absolutely no way I can get past them, and I also know that I won't be able to get the front door open, so I start looking around as I try to figure out where I can go next. I refuse to believe that after getting out of the ropes and making my way up from the basement, I'm trapped all over again.

"Relax," Nick is saying casually, "I'll take care of that too. I've got a total plan in place, and you don't have to worry about any of it. Just do *what* I tell you, *when* I tell you, and it'll be fine."

"What about the cop?" Alex asks. "We can't just leave him in the bedroom."

"Who said anything about leaving him in the bedroom? We're gonna get him out of here before we call anyone."

"What will you do to him?"

"That's for me to worry about."

"But -"

"Well, and him. He should be worried too."

"What exactly are you going to do?"

"Chill, Alex," he continues, interrupting her. "I'll deal with the cop *and* Maddie."

"Do you have to hurt Maddie?" she asks, sounding a little hesitant. "I mean, she hasn't really done anything wrong. She had good intentions, anyway. Can't we just, like, let her go?"

"Don't ask me questions like that," he replies.

"Maybe we can talk her round."

"I'm taking this off your hands so that you don't have to worry about it," he continues. "That was the deal, remember? I'll do the tough stuff, and in return you have to promise not to ask about all the pesky details. I guarantee I'll sort it, but don't keep nagging. Your job is to get all those old books together and figure out how we're gonna present this to people. I also need you to get a camera from somewhere." He lets out a loud sigh. "We're gonna have one more of these blunts each," he adds finally, "and then we're getting back to work."

Backing away from the door, I realize that I'm trapped in the house. At the same time, it sounds like they're going to be out there for at least ten minutes, so I start trying to figure out if there's any other way to leave. I could try forcing open one of the boarded-up windows, but I'm pretty sure that'd make too much noise. After a moment, however, I remember the window in one of the bedrooms, where a section of one board has already started to come away. If I could wriggle out through *that* and then somehow drop down at the front of the house, I might be able to get to the street and find help.

The whole idea seems crazy, but right now it's all I've got.

As Alex and Nick continue to talk, I turn and carefully make my way toward the stairs, and then I head up toward the landing. With each step, I'm terrified that there'll be a loud creaking sound, but miraculously I reach the top and see that the doors to the bedrooms have been left open. I make my way carefully to the nearest, and sure enough I see that one of the boards has an opening that would allow me to get out.

I glance over my shoulder, to double-check that there's no sign of Alex or Nick coming inside, and then I head over to the door. At the last moment, however, I stop as I see a pair of legs on the floor in another room, poking into view from behind the door of the second bedroom.

"Matt?" I whisper, before heading over and looking inside. "Matt, are -"

I let out a shocked gasp as soon as I see him. He's on the floor, tied to the bed, and his unconscious face has been badly beaten. There's blood everywhere, and his skin looks to have been split open in several places. I hurry over to him and drop to my knees, but I'm scared to touch him in case I make anything worse.

"Matt, can you hear me?" I ask, trying not to panic. "Matt, say something!"

When he doesn't respond, I reach out and press two fingers against the side of his bloodied neck. At first I don't feel any sign of life, but after a moment I'm just about able to detect a heartbeat. He's alive, but I'm not sure he's going to stay that way for long, not without help.

"Why did they do this to you?" I whisper, before realizing that this must be Nick's work.

And if he's willing to go this far, there's no telling what else he might do. All my worst fears are coming true: Nick's a psychopath.

"I'm going to get you out of here," I continue. "I

don't know if you can hear me, but I'm going to get us *both* out of here, but I have to go and get help, okay?"

Even as I say those words, however, I know that there's no way I can carry him with me. I don't want to leave him behind, but I figure that my only option is to get out of the house and go for help, and then pray to God that I get back in time with the police. So long as Alex and Nick don't realize that I've made it out of the basement, I at least have a chance. And if I have a chance, then Matt has one too.

"I'll be back," I tell Matt, although I doubt he can hear me at all. "I'm not leaving you behind. I mean, I'm leaving, but only to get help. I'll be quick, I swear."

I wait, just in case he's able to say anything, and then I lean forward so I can kiss his forehead. Getting to my feet, I hurry to the window and drop back down onto my knees, and then I start trying to push the broken board a little further out of the way. The gap turns out to be not quite large enough for me to crawl out, but the board feels pretty loose so I think I have a chance if I can just force it a little further. The problem, though, is that I can't afford to make too much noise. I can already see the street outside, but I know that if I call for help I'll end up letting Alex and Nick know that I'm free. Even if I managed to get away after that, there'd be a danger that they might do more to Matt.

I have to stay quiet and get out of here fast.

Still struggling with the board, I have to start pushing with my shoulder. This causes a very faint rattling noise, but I guess that's okay so long as the others are all the way round at the rear of the house. The board doesn't seem to be coming loose very easily, however, and I'm starting to worry that I might need to try another option. Reaching up, I feel several nails that are still holding everything in place, and pulling at their heads doesn't seem to help. Still, for now all I can do is try to firmly – but quietly – break the board open, even though so far I don't seem to be making any progress at all. I turn and put my shoulder against one corner, and then I start -

Suddenly I hear footsteps downstairs, and the sound of voices as Alex and Nick come back inside. A moment later, I hear them starting to come upstairs.

CHAPTER THIRTEEN
DOCTOR CHARLES GRAZIER

Thursday October 4th, 1888

Finally she falls still.

***

SOBBING, BLEEDING PROFUSELY from wounds around my chest and abdomen and waist, I drag myself through the open doorway and into the main part of the basement. I've already split several fingernails against the rough floor, and I'm trembling terribly with fear and pain, but finally I feel my feet bumping against the frame of the door. I haul myself a little further, and then I turn and look back into the storage room.

I let out a shocked gasp as soon as I see her.

Catherine – or the thing that masquerades as Catherine – is slumped in the darkness. Her furious attack lasted for several minutes, but eventually she seemed to tire. As soon as she slithered off me, I began to drag myself free, although I was convinced at first that she would come at me again, at any moment. The fact that I have made it out here is a miracle but, as I continue to watch her, I see that she is already turning once more to look at me.

"No!" I gasp, somehow finding the strength to get on my knees. I grab the door and swing it shut, sealing her once more inside the room. "No, please no..."

I'm shaking so much, I can barely slide the bolt back into place or turn the key, but finally the door is secured. Sliding down, I feel as if I shall never again muster the strength to move. I have lost so much blood, and I cannot even begin to count my wounds. Indeed, I believe I lost all awareness during the worst of her attack, although now I look down at my body and see that there is blood caked all around my waist and groin. What did she do to me? Why did she want?

I have to end this. Finally, I have to do the right thing.

***

"Inspector Sanderson please!" I say firmly, as I wait at the Scotland Yard desk. "I will speak to Sanderson, and only Sanderson."

"And what is this about, Sir?" the indolent lackey asks.

"I shall tell him when I see him!" I reply, no longer able to hide my impatience. I am in excruciating pain, and even the simple task of standing here is almost too much for my trembling legs. "It's getting late, man, and I endured the most frightful ride over here. Please, get Inspector Sanderson so that I can speak to him. It's about a very important matter."

"But -"

"It's about Jack the Ripper!"

The young fool opens his mouth to reply, but then he hesitates.

"Bear with me one moment, please," he says, getting to his feet. "I'll return presently."

"See that you do," I say with a sigh, "and see that you have Inspector Sanderson with you."

As he hurries through to another room, I am left standing along in the corridor. It is late, and I scarcely managed to get here tonight. I cleaned my wounds as best I could, and bandaged them, and then I changed into these fresh clothes. So far no blood has soaked through, but I am sure that will happen eventually. And then, even after I made it to my front door, I found that those pale young ladies were still waiting outside. I hurried past them, however, and quickly hailed a carriage. Now that I am here at Scotland Yard, I am finally ready to confess everything. Catherine is gone, and all that remains of her is a foul husk that sits trapped in my basement. The real Catherine waits for me in death, and I shall go to her soon, but first...

First I must confess everything.

After all, if Catherine knows what I have done, she will surely be horrified. Indeed, the only thing I can do now is face justice, and hope that this proves to

Catherine that I remain at heart the good man she married. I will even hang, if that is what it takes. Of course, for any of this to happen, I first need to actually see Inspector Sanderson and tell him what has happened. I suppose he will want proof, but proof is waiting in the basement of my home. I can give him all the proof he needs.

Besides, he knows.

I am sure of it now.

All that talk of Doctor Culpepper was just a distraction, a way to test my responses. Sanderson cannot possibly believe that Culpepper is responsible. I am quite certain that he suspects me, that he has perhaps even been watching my every move for some time. Soon the whole world will know that I, Doctor Charles Grazier, am Jack the Ripper. My name shall live forever. I can only hope that my motivations are understood.

"Hello?" I call out, frustrated that the idiot deskboy has still not returned. I bang the tip of my cane against the table, yet still there is no sign of Sanderson coming to speak to me. "I demand an answer!" I shout. "This is intolerable! I want to speak to Mr. Sanderson at once!"

Yet still there is no reply.

"What is the world coming to?" I mutter under my breath, but then a moment later I hear footsteps at the far end of the corridor.

Turning, I see that a man is walking this way, with the desk lackey right behind him. I step forward, relieved that I shall finally be able to tell Sanderson everything, but then I realize that the man is somebody else entirely.

"Where is Sanderson?" I ask, unable to hide my anger. "If he's not here, have a man sent to wake him up! I know it's late, but I don't care. I must speak to him at once!"

"My name is Hargreaves," the man says, reaching out to shake my hand. "Might I be of assistance?"

"I shall speak only to Inspector Sanderson," I reply, conspicuously keeping my hand away from him. I do not want him to feel my weakness. "It must be Sanderson."

"So I'm told," this Hargreaves fellow continues, "but I'm afraid there's simply nobody here by that name."

"Then have him brought from home!"

I wait, but the imbecile merely stares at me.

"Fetch him!" I roar, flinching as I feel a stabbing pain in my crotch. "Do it!"

He sighs.

"You will fetch him," I sneer, feeling a little breathless now, "or I swear..."

"There is nobody at Scotland Yard by the name of Sanderson!" he says with another sigh. "I've double-checked. There's a Sanders, and a Saunders, but no Sanderson." He hesitates for a moment, eyeing me with suspicion. "Might *I* be able to help you, Sir?"

"Of course there's a Sanderson," I stammer, although I must confess that I am starting to feel a little dizzy. "I was here with him earlier."

"I hardly think that's possible," he replies.

"I was here!" I snap. "He took me to the room where they keep all the dead girls!"

"And what room would that be?"

"The room with the bodies!" I continue, exasperated by his idiocy. "There were scores of them laid out on tables! The victims of Jack the Ripper, and other girls who'd been murdered too! They're all in a big room so that they can be examined!"

"We have no such room," Hargreaves replies. "Are you sure that you were in *this* building?"

"Of course I was! What nonsense is this? Why can I not speak to Sanderson? I was with him earlier, and he told me all about his theory regarding Doctor Thomas Culpepper!"

"Perhaps we should go and take a seat somewhere," Hargreaves says, and now he sounds a little hesitant, as if he's worried about me. "I'm told that you might have information concerning the Ripper case. I happen to be involved with that investigation, so I should very much like to hear what you have to tell us. We get a lot of people coming to us with their theories, but seldom gentlemen such as yourself. I should like to -"

"He's not real!" I gasp, taking a step back. "I spoke to him! I walked with him on multiple occasions! Can I possibly have been so deluded, so out of my mind, that I imagined the whole thing, stretching back..."

My voice trails off, and for a moment I think of the very first time I encountered Sanderson.

"I'm so very sorry to have disturbed you at your home," he told me, barely three days ago. "I also know,

Sir, that you recently retired. It's just that we're badly in need of some additional expertise and, well, Doctor Brown mentioned you as somebody who could be relied upon to render an expert opinion."

Could that have all been in my mind?

"How about we speak somewhere more private?" Hargreaves asks, suddenly placing a hand on my arm. "You can start by telling us your name, and then we can go from there. If you have information about the Ripper -"

"I have no information about anything!" I snap, pulling away from him. "I must get home. I no longer know what is real and what is a figment of my imagination."

Did I even say those words? As I take another step back, these two gentlemen stare at me as if I am completely insane, yet they do not specifically respond to what I said. Sweat is starting to run down my face, and I am suddenly gripped by the realization that I must get out of here. In fact, it is starting to become clear that Inspector Hargreaves and his dumb little friend are eyeing me with the kind of suspicion that one would usually reserve for a suspect. I have said too much, and I must get home as quickly as possible.

And then, quite suddenly, I see Sanderson standing right behind them, staring at me with malevolent intensity.

"Do you see him?" I ask.

"I beg your pardon, Sir?" Hargreaves replies.

"Right behind you," I continue. "Do you see him?"

He and the lackey both turn and look around. They must surely be able to see Inspector Sanderson, yet after a moment they turn to me with expressions of pure incomprehension.

"Who, Sir?" Hargreaves asks. "Who are we supposed to see?"

"Good evening," I mumble, turning and hurrying away.

"Wait!" Hargreaves calls out. "I want to hear what you have to say!"

Pushing the door open, I hurry out into the night and then slip down a side-alley. A moment later I hear the door opening again, and I pull back into the shadows as I see Hargreaves and his friend rushing out and stopping at the top of the steps. They seem keen to find me, but thankfully they do not think to come and look for me here, so I simply wait until they start heading back inside.

"Did you catch the gentleman's name?" Hargreaves asks, and to my immense relief his colleague answers in the negative.

Still, I wait several more minutes, until I am certain that the coast is clear. Then I head out past the end of the alley and make my way along the street, while constantly checking over my shoulder to make sure that I am not being followed. I feel utterly out of sorts, and I am quite certain that I must have seemed rather strange to those two police officers. At the same time, I know that they did not get my name, and they will most likely dismiss me as just one of the many madmen who populate London's streets at night.

Now I must get home and deal with the creature in the basement. And then I must finally make my way to Catherine and join her in paradise. I have sworn that before, of course, but this time I shall let nothing stand in my way.

CHAPTER FOURTEEN
MADDIE

Today

"NAH, HE'S STILL OUT FOR THE COUNT," Nick mutters, almost sounding bored as he towers over Matt's unconscious body. He gives him a kick in the shoulders before turning and shuffling out of the bedroom. "He'll be lucky if he ever wakes up. Or unlucky."

Holding my breath, too terrified to make even the slightest sound, I stay hidden under the bed as I listen to Nick going through to the next room. I still have the knife in my right hand, clutched tight, although I know it wouldn't be much use if I had to actually defend myself. Fortunately, Nick and Alex seem far more interested in looking through the drawers in the bedroom, and they're taking their sweet time. They also keep stopping to get a little physical with each other, which makes me feel sick to my stomach but which at least delays them going back to the basement. Eventually they're going to figure out that I'm free, however, and I'm not sure I'll be able to get out the window in time.

"Come on," I hear Nick say in the other room, "we haven't done it in here yet."

"Shouldn't we be getting on with this?" Alex asks.

"There's not much more we can do until it gets dark," he replies. "Seriously, we need to celebrate. We're sorted for life. This time tomorrow, you'll see that I've get everything figured out. So how about right now, we have some fun?"

I wait, and a moment later I hear the sound of them fumbling together. They're having sex again, and they're being pretty loud about it too. I desperately want to get out of here, but I can't take the risk that they'd see me if I tried to sneak past. Even if I somehow managed to run, Matt would be left behind and I don't think there are any limits to what Nick would do to him then. Still barely daring to breathe, I listen to the increasingly loud sounds of Nick and Alex in the other room, and I -

Suddenly a hand clamps tight against my mouth. Terrified, I try to pull away, but the hand is too tight and then a moment later I turn and see that Matt – bruised and bloodied, and with one of his eyes swollen shut – has finally come around.

He puts a finger against his lips, to remind me to keep quiet, and then slowly he moves his hand away from my mouth.

"What are you doing here?" he whispers finally, as the noise from the other room continues.

"I got out of the basement," I reply, keeping my voice low, "and I came to find you."

"Are you insane?" he hisses. "You should have run and got help!"

"I couldn't! They were right outside!"

"Listen to me," he continues, "I'm too badly hurt to get out of here. You have to go, Maddie. Do you understand? It has to be you."

"I can't," I tell him, as tears run down my face. "Please, I can't go out there..."

"You have to. It's our only shot."

"I was going to get the window open and climb out."

"So why didn't you?" he asks.

"I couldn't get the board out of the way."

"Then your only option is to get down those stairs and out the door."

"I can't!"

"If you don't, we'll die here!" he says firmly.

I shake my head.

"Do you think they're bluffing?" he asks. "Look at me, Maddie! I don't know what their plan is, but it's a miracle we're not both dead already."

"Alex wouldn't do that," I sob. "Maybe I can talk to her. Maybe I can make her see that this is all crazy."

"I don't know a damn thing about your friend Alex," he replies, "but that guy in there? He's dangerous, and right now I think he's in charge around here. I don't think Alex is going to stand up to him, so you have to get out of here and call someone, okay?" He pauses, before reaching out and placing a hand on my shoulder. "I know you can do it, Maddie. You're tougher than you realize."

Again, I shake my head.

"You don't have a choice!" he continues. "What else are you going to do? Are you going to hide here until they realize you escaped? Or until they come in and find you? You can't hide forever!"

"But Alex -"

"You can't trust her, Maddie!"

"I can't go out there alone," I reply. "Please don't make me..."

"You can and you will!" he says firmly. "Maddie, it sounds like they're having fun all by themselves, but that won't last much longer. You have to get out there right now. Once you've reached the stairs, if I hear that they might be finished I'll cause a distraction."

"They'll kill you!"

"I'll cause a distraction," he says again, "and you have to run. Don't worry about me, okay? I can take care of myself. If you'd found a way to get out the first time, help would be on the way by now. Maddie, you're the only one who can get us out of here. I need you to do this." He squeezes my shoulder tight. "I know you can do it."

"What if they see me?" I whimper.

"Then you have to run."

"But -"

"And don't look back. You have to be brave."

"I'm not brave!"

"Yeah, you are. You're very brave. But if it comes down to it, you have to run and get help."

I open my mouth to tell him that I can't do any of this, but somehow the words dry in the back of my throat. At the same time, I can hear that Nick and Alex are getting close to finishing, and suddenly I realize that Matt is right: I have to find a way out of the house. If I stay here, we're both going to die, and it'll be all my fault. I'm the one who called Matt and asked him to come here, and I'm the one who didn't realize that Nick and Alex were so dangerous. Even if the odds of success are low, I have to do whatever I can. Turning and looking toward the open door, I see the top of the stairs and I finally understand that I don't have a choice.

"I'll be quick," I whisper, turning back to Matt. "I'll get help, I swear!"

"Go!" he whispers, letting go of my shoulder and pushing me away. "Run, Maddie! Don't look back!"

I want to tell him that he'll be fine, but I know that I'm only delaying things. Getting to my feet, I hesitate for a moment before leaning down and placing the knife next to Matt's hand.

"No!" he hisses. "Take it! You need it!"

"You need it more," I reply. "If they spot me, I can try to run. You can't."

"Take the knife!" he replies, but I start making my way toward the door. As I get closer, I can tell that Nick and Alex are almost done, but I don't dare go too much faster. I glance back at Matt and see the fear in his eyes, and then I slip out onto the landing.

I can do this.

My heart is racing, but I know I can do this.

I'm -

"Damn!" Nick yells suddenly, and I hear footsteps in the next bedroom.

Startled, I duck down behind the landing table, just as Nick comes storming out of the room and starts hurrying down the stairs.

"Hey, come back!" Alex shouts after him. "It's okay! It's not a big deal!"

He doesn't reply. Instead, I hear him heading into one of the downstairs rooms and slamming the door shut. At least he didn't go to the basement, and I figure I still have a shot of getting out of here. I check over my shoulder, to make sure that there's no sign of Alex, and then I crawl out from behind the table and over toward the top of the stairs. I stop for a few seconds, listening to make sure that Nick isn't coming back, and then I get to my feet.

"Maddie?" Alex says suddenly, right behind me. Reaching out, she grabs my wrist tight. "Where the hell do you think *you're* going?"

CHAPTER FIFTEEN
DOCTOR CHARLES GRAZIER

Thursday October 4th, 1888

I push Delilah's cold, lifeless corpse off the slab and send her crashing to the floor. I shall dispose of her later, but for now I have other work to finish.

***

I CAN HEAR HER DOWN THERE, still trying to break through the door in the basement. It's evident that she has not managed to get through just yet, but it is also clear that sooner or later she will achieve some degree of success.

And then what?

I must do *something*, yet I cannot begin to imagine how I shall stop her. The most obvious solution would be to somehow take her body apart, to undo the work I have done, but I am not sure that I can summon sufficient strength. Then again, perhaps fire would be a better option. I could set the basement ablaze and burn the whole house down. In some ways, that would seem to be the most appropriate course of action, yet I am not sure I could bear to hear her screams.

Stepping toward the door that leads down into the basement, I hesitate for a moment before stopping again as I realize that I cannot go down there yet, I just cannot.

Slowly, I turn and look up the stairs. I must ask for guidance.

***

I swore I would never do this. I swore I would never kill a child. Yet now, in the palm of my hand...

***

"Are you here?" I ask, standing in the doorway that leads into the main bedroom. "Catherine, can you hear me? I know now that the thing in the basement is not you, but I must... Are you here?"

I feel so utterly foolish, but at the same time I cannot hold back. If there is even the slightest chance that Catherine is here in this room, in some manner that perhaps I do not understand, then I have to attempt to make contact with her. And whereas I have delayed this moment for several days now, I know now that I can delay no longer. This nightmare must end tonight.

I do not want to believe in something so common as a ghost, yet I have no choice.

"I know that I have become a bad man," I explain, stepping forward and removing my spectacles, so as to reveal my torn eyelids. "Perhaps I am not even the man that you married. Not really. In truth, I no longer know who or what I am, and I rely entirely upon your judgment. Can you not come to me and speak? I should very much like to die knowing whether you will accept me in the next world."

I wait, but the room remains silent. I can still hear, however, the sound of that *thing* still trying to break out from the storage room in the basement.

"I shall destroy her in a moment," I continue. "I do not know how, but I shall find a way. Even if I have to hack her apart with an ax, or burn the house to the ground, I promise you that she will not persist beyond this night. Yet before I do any of that, I must know whether you are here. Do you survive in spirit, Catherine? Is such a thing possible?"

Please be possible.

Again I wait.

Again, I hear no reply.

"Just one thing," I whisper. "I have braved ghosts in the streets tonight, so I am certain that I can brave one more. Do not recoil from me, my darling. Show yourself."

Staring at the empty bed, I wait for a moment before stepping closer. I wish I could say that I sense Catherine's presence, that somehow I know she is close; in truth, however, the room feels utterly abandoned, and

I cannot fool myself. Perhaps a lesser man could let his guard down and make all sorts of outlandish claims, but at heart I am still a man of science and I know full well that I have neither heard nor felt any evidence of Catherine's presence. Nothing beyond desperate hallucinations, at least.

After all, if I could imagine a police inspector, and hallucinate whole trips to Scotland Yard, then I could most certainly fool myself into thinking that I detected hints of my dead wife in this room.

"I have been a fool," I whisper finally. "I have told myself over and over again that I am on the brink of a breakthrough, yet there has been no breakthrough. I was a wise man once, but I have allowed myself to -"

"Charles," Catherine's voice whispers.

I freeze, staring down at the floor. I must have imagined that voice, I cannot have heard it, yet it seemed so utterly real. I am sure, however, that -

"Charles, come with me," she says suddenly.

I look toward the bed, and I am shocked to see her sitting in plain sight. She is staring at me, watching me with her usual smile, and she looks as healthy and as happy as I recall from the days before she was sick. There is a faint glow to her, too, as if she is not entirely of this world. For a moment, I can only stare at her with a sense of wonder.

"You *are* still a good man," she continues. "I know that. Despite everything you have done, I know that you still have a good heart. You have done bad things, but out of love for me, and I know that your soul remains strong. Trust me, there is no judgment in the next life, at least not beyond that which you pass down upon yourself. I can help you, but I think..."

She pauses, and I think I see tears in her eyes.

"Oh my darling," she says finally, "forgive me, but I think it's time for you to join me now."

"This is not real," I whisper, thinking back to all the things I have imagined. "Such miracles cannot be bestowed upon man."

"Come with me right now," she continues, reaching a hand out toward me. "Don't wait a moment longer, Charles. I wanted you to live without me, but now I can see that your life is drawing to an end. By the time this night is over, you will have left the land of the living and we shall be together forever."

"No," I say, taking a step back. "You are not really here. This is all a trick, designed to draw me even deeper into madness. You are nothing more than a cheap parlor trick."

"Follow my lead, Charles. Do not overthink this. Instead, take my hand and come to me in the world that follows this. We can be together, and we can leave this mortal place forever. You have done terrible things, but there are ways to atone. I can help you. You need me, do you not?"

"If I believed you were real," I reply, "I would at this moment be the happiest man who ever lived. I would dearly love to throw myself into this fantasy, yet I must hold back. I have imagined so many things, including my own brilliance, and now at the end I must cling to some semblance of reality."

With that, I step back and pull the door shut.

"You're making a mistake!" she calls out. "I've finally broken through to speak to you, Charles. You didn't realize at the time, but you were pushing me away. Now you're ready to understand, but you need to listen properly. Charles, please!"

Listen?

I shall not listen to this phantom that has been summoned from the depths of my mind. I shall not allow myself to be fooled again, especially not by my own delusions. I am a better man than that, and the real Catherine would most certainly be horrified if she could see me now. I know that the vision on the bed was merely a hallucination, and that I am completely alone here in the house, and I feel that I have finally found the strength to push this madness away. Despite all the insanity that has gripped me, I insist upon dying with a clear mind.

Indeed, I no longer hear Catherine's voice coming from the other side of the door. As I back away toward the top of the stairs, I feel some degree of satisfaction at the thought that at least I have conquered these fears. Now I must simply deal with the last of my affairs, and settle a few outstanding matters, and then I shall do what I should have done last week. I am finally ready to meet my fate. I must leave behind a confession, and then I must burn this house to the ground so that nothing can ever again disturb its evil. And this time, I shall let nothing stand in my way.

"Doctor Grazier."

Startled, I turn and look down the stairs.

"I have returned," Jack says calmly, staring up at

me with an unusual intensity in his gaze. "Where is Delilah?"

CHAPTER SIXTEEN
MADDIE

Today

"YOU DUMB LITTLE BITCH," Alex whispers, keeping her voice down as if she doesn't want Nick to hear us from downstairs. "Do you seriously think you can get out of here?"

Backing away, I bump against the wall. All I can think right now is that I have to somehow draw her away from Matt.

"I was going to help you!" she continues, stepping toward me. "I wasn't going to let him hurt you, Maddie. Not properly. Come on, do you seriously think I'd let anything happen to my little Maddie? I know that what Nick and I did was bad, but I had no idea he could get like that. He can be extreme sometimes, but I didn't realize he was going to actually hurt people. He even told me..."

Her voice trails off for a moment.

"Please," I whimper, still trying to figure out what to do next. "Alex, I have to get help."

"He killed someone already," she replies, and I think I can see fear in her eyes.

"What do you mean?" I ask.

Suddenly pulls me into one of the bedrooms. Glancing past me for a moment, she seems terrified that Nick might overhear us.

"He told me," she continues finally, lowering her voice as she turns to me. "He killed one of the girls who was found dead in the streets, one of the girls who was supposed to have been killed by a Jack the Ripper copycat. He says that's how it is now, he says there's not *one* killer out there, it's more of an initiation rite. He fell in with these assholes who worship Jack the Ripper, and they each have to commit one murder in his style in order to join the group. Nick killed some girl on Vauxhall Road, and now I think..."

Her voice trails off for a moment.

"I think he's lying to me," she adds finally. "He says we're going to get rich from this place, but then he keeps stalling, he keeps saying we have to wait until it gets dark but he doesn't say why. None of what he says or does makes sense, not unless... I think he's going to get other people to come here, people who are like him. Maddie, I'm scared of Nick and I don't know what to do. He's violent, he gets really mad sometimes. He makes me do things, and I can't stop myself. I even hurt *you*, and I hate that so much. He just gets into my head and changes the way I think!"

"Funny," I reply, "he said the same thing about you."

"I swear," she continues, "he's so good at manipulating people. He's made me do bad things, Maddie, really bad things. Things you don't even know about. I'm scared he'll hurt me. I'm scared he'll hurt us all!"

"Then let's leave," I tell her. "Let's go and get help."

"He won't let us."

"I don't care whether he'll *let* us!" I reply, starting to worry that this is taking too much time, that maybe she's trying to delay me so that Nick will eventually come back. "Alex, you have to come with me! We'll get help and -"

"I'll keep him busy," she says suddenly, stepping back from me.

"Alex -"

"I'll distract him and make sure he doesn't see you leaving," she continues, "and then I'll try to keep him busy until you can get back with help. He gets in my head, Maddie. He makes me think differently, he makes me do things I'd never normally do. Please, you have to get out of here before he does it again, 'cause I'm scared I might betray you again. As soon as I get him out of the way, you have to run!"

I open my mouth to tell her that we need to go together, but suddenly I hear a door opening downstairs.

"Hey!" Nick calls out. "Alex, baby! Why don't we go down and check on little Maddie?"

Alex gestures for me to wait a moment, and then

she turns and starts heading down the stairs.

"Sorry," she says to Nick as she reaches the hallway, "I just had to fix myself up first."

"Who were you talking to?"

Dropping to my knees, I crawl around the side of the table until I can just about see them down there. My heart is pounding and I have no idea whether I can trust Alex, but I guess right now I don't have a choice.

"I wasn't talking to anyone," she says, although she sounds scared. "I was singing to myself. Maybe you heard that." She steps past him and opens the door to the basement. "Come on, why don't we go down together?"

"It didn't sound like you were singing," Nick replies cautiously, and it's clear that he's suspicious. "It sounded like you were whispering."

"I checked if that cop was awake," she explains. "He wasn't. You really beat him to a pulp, yeah? I'm not even sure he'll *ever* come around." Holding the basement door open, she waits for him to join her. "Why don't we both go down to the basement and check on Maddie? She's been down there for hours now, she's probably losing her mind."

She waits for a reply, but now Nick is simply staring at her.

"I want to check on Maddie," she says again, and now she sounds really nervous. "Can we just do that?"

"Why the hurry?"

"I want to make sure she doesn't find some way to get out of those ropes," she continues. "Trust me, I know her pretty well, and she's smart. If there's any way to get loose, she'll find it. She's sneakier than she looks." She hesitates for a moment, as if she's waiting for him to say something. "She's brave, too," she adds. "You don't know her like I do, but Maddie's brave and she always finds a way. That's one of the things I admire the most about her. I know that no matter what happens, she'll always manage to get through."

Again she waits, and again Nick says nothing.

"Fine," he replies finally, "then go take a look."

"Let's go together."

"Why?"

"What if she's loose and she attacks me?"

"Then fight her off," he says with a shrug. "She's not as big as you, Alex. You can take her."

"I'd really rather we went down together," she explains. She's sounding less and less convincing all the time, but I just have to hope that she manages to persuade Nick. If I'm lucky, she might even be planning to trap him down there. "Is that such a problem?" she adds. "I mean, don't you think it'd be fun to give her a kicking? You were laughing while you were beating that cop senseless."

He hesitates, before stepping over toward her.

"You know we're in this together, right?" he asks after a moment.

"Of course, but -"

"And we're on the same side." Stopping, he puts a hand on the side of her face. "That means we tell each other everything. No secrets, no lies, just good old-fashioned honesty and truth." He pauses, staring into her eyes. "We're a team here, Alex," he continues finally.

"Five minutes ago, up in that bedroom, I proved to you that I know how you work. I know how your mind functions, and I'm getting a pretty good idea about your body too. Now, I think you might be right, we should probably go and check to make sure Maddie's still tied up in the basement. First, though, I want you to think about whether there's anything you haven't told me. Anything at all."

"Like what?" she stammers.

"If I knew, I wouldn't need to ask." He pauses again. "Are you hiding something from me, Alex?"

"Of course not!"

"You're not keeping any little secrets?"

He waits for an answer, and for a moment I worry that she might be about to rat me out. After all, she told me that Nick can get into her mind and manipulate her, and maybe that's what's happening right now.

"I don't know where you're getting all this stuff from," Maddie stammers finally, "but let's just go and check on Maddie, okay? Why would I want to go check on her, if I was hiding anything? We're totally on the same side, Nick, so just relax. We'll check on Maddie, and then we'll go do whatever you want. We can kill that cop, if you like. That's what you're planning to do to him, right?"

He pauses. "Yeah," he says after a moment. "Sure."

"And Maddie too?"

"Why not?" he asks. "If I'm gonna have to dig a hole in the garden, makes no difference whether I throw one body down there or two."

"Then let's go," she says, tugging on his arm.

"Or three bodies," he adds.

"What?"

She stares at him, and even from up here I can see the fear reaching her eyes.

"Nick," she continues, "what do -"

Suddenly he steps closer, and Alex lets out a pained gasp. It takes a moment before I realize that Nick's right arm is twitching, and a moment later I see blood dribbling down onto the floor between Alex's legs. Then, when Nick steps back, I see that he's holding a knife.

"No!" I yell, getting to my feet. "Alex! Run!"

Nick stabs her again and again, driving the blade into her belly and chest so many times that I start hearing a loud squelching sound. Alex looks up at me, her eyes filled with horror, but a moment later she tries to push Nick away. Her knees buckle, however, and Nick simply shoves her back toward the open doorway. She looks at me again, and I think she tries to say something, but then she topples backward and falls from view, and I hear the sickening sound of her body crashing down the steps until it slams into the concrete at the bottom.

"That's one out of the way," Nick says with a smile, before turning and looking up toward me. In his hand, he's holding some kind of bloodied lump that he tore from Alex's body. He watches me for a moment, before making his way across the hallway and starting to come up the stairs, with the bloodied knife still in his hand. "Just two more to go."

CHAPTER SEVENTEEN
DOCTOR CHARLES GRAZIER

Thursday October 4th, 1888

"WHERE IS SHE?" Jack sneers, grabbing my lapels and slamming me against the wall at the bottom of the main staircase. "What have you done to her?"

All I can do is stare at him, as I try to determine whether or not he is really here. I can feel him pressing me into the wall, yet I also know that I have imagined so many things over the past few days. I no longer trust myself to determine what is real and what is not, and I fear very much that perhaps Jack's sudden return is just the latest in a long list of imagined occurrences. Perhaps he is one final obstacle that I must overcome before I burn this house down.

"I thought you were gone for good," I gasp, barely able to breathe as he tightens his grip. "Then again, perhaps you were never real in the first place."

"Never real?" he asks, leaning closer. "Are you serious?"

"Perhaps you are an illusion," I continue, "and -"

Before I can finish, he punches me hard in the gut. When he lets go of me, I slump down to the floor, wincing with pain as I struggle to get my breath back. Rolling onto my side, I let out a pained groan.

"Did that feel real?" he asks.

I try to get to my feet, but the pain is too strong.

"You sent me to run errands," he continues, towering over me, "but I very nearly never came back. I took myself back to the slums of the city, I tried to bury myself in my old life, yet I could not forget everything that I left behind here. Every time I thought of Delilah, I realized that I had left her in your care, and finally I came to realize that I could not in good conscience abandon her so. I know that you have not simply sent her away, so I demand that you tell me the truth. For your sake, I hope that you have not hurt her."

Reaching down, he grabs me by the collar and hauls me half up until our faces are almost touching.

"WHERE IS SHE?"

Before I can respond, my spectacles fall away and I immediately see the shock in Jack's eyes.

"What has happened to you?" he asks, his voice filled with a growing sense of horror. "You look..."

His voice trails off, and finally he lets go of me and takes a step back.

"What *has* happened to you?" he asks again. "Never have I seen a man crumble so greatly. I have been gone for two days, Doctor Grazier, and in that time you appear to have fallen apart."

"I have been busy," I reply, adjusting my collar. "You cannot possibly understand the depths of my work. Then again, perhaps you were designed that way. After all, it is highly likely that you are merely an imagining."

"Where is Delilah?"

Shaking my head, I start limping through to my office.

"Tell me," he continues, walking after me. "Is she resting in bed? She *is* here, is she not?"

There is no point speaking to this illusion, so I merely make my way over to my desk and begin to take a look at my notebooks. My hands are shaking violently, for some reason that I cannot quite determine, but I still feel that I should be able to focus my thoughts and recover my sanity. I am Doctor Charles Grazier, distinguished member of no less than five London societies. I am respected by my peers and regarded as one of the finest surgeons of my generation and I refuse to let my mind fall apart in this manner. Not again. At the end, I shall be myself again.

"All that matters is my work," I say out loud as I continue to sort through the notebooks, although I am shocked by the fragile sound of my voice. "I must dedicate myself to -"

"Where is Delilah?"

I flinch at the sound of his voice, but I immediately remind myself that he is not real, and that I will only strengthen the illusion if I respond to him in any way. I am tempted to glance at him, of course, but I manage to fight the urge and to instead focus on the notebooks.

"I once thought that you were a great man," he continues. "I thought that you merely needed help, in order that you would return to your work. But then the doubts came and settled in my mind, and I began to understand that you were suffering from some kind of mania. I very nearly did not return to this house at all, Doctor Grazier, and I would not have done so if I had not begun to worry about Delilah. I watched her home, waiting to see if she would return. She did not, so I can only assume that she remains here. Let me take her, Doctor Grazier. I know that you would not have harmed a woman while she carries a child, I know that harming a child was the one line you refused to cross, so let me take her and then we shall never return. Nor shall we speak of this to others. We'll simply leave you be."

"Now where was that page?" I mutter to myself, leafing through the notebook. In truth, I am not looking for anything in particular; rather, I am simply attempting to focus my mind.

"I shall find her," Jack says with a sigh, turning and walking out of the room.

"She is gone," I reply, before I am able to stop myself.

His boots squeak as he stops in his tracks.

I turn slightly, almost looking at him. My eyes are sore and damaged, and I perceive only the faintest shadow of a man standing in the doorway, before I look down at the notebooks and try to focus on my old work. Barely able to see properly, I lean closer in an attempt to decipher my own handwriting, but my eyesight is beginning to fail me. Is this how I am to die? Not only mad, but blind too?

"Gone where?" Jack asks, and now there is fear in his voice.

"I used to collect women from the streets and bring them here," I reply, unable to hold back any longer. Perhaps it will do me some good to talk to this illusion. "Now I take women from my home and leave them on the streets. Delilah Culpepper was -"

"Did you harm her?" he asks, interrupting me.

"She was very useful."

"I swear," he continues, "that if you have hurt her in any manner, I shall make you pay."

"Catherine needed her," I reply, "and so the woman served her purpose. If I did not know better, I -"

Before I can finish, my right leg suddenly gives way. I fall down onto my knee, letting out a gasp of pain as I land, and it takes a moment for me to steady myself against the table. I cannot comprehend how or why, but it is as if my body is beginning to fail me. Letting out a faint murmur, I take a few seconds to regather my strength, and then I haul myself back to my feet. I feel desperately unsteady, as if I might fall again at any moment, and it is perhaps for the best that I am entirely alone here.

Yes, I am alone.

There is no Jack.

Perhaps there never was. It has all been about me, all along, and Jack was merely a pitiful fragment of my own mind. He was my mind's way of coping with its own troubles, and -

Suddenly I hear him storming out of the room, and the floorboards shudder slightly beneath my feet. A moment later I hear the basement door swing open, and I turn just in time to see him heading down into the darkness.

"Wait!" I blurt out, before remembering that he is not real, before realizing that perhaps he is after all, before reminding myself that I am a strong man, before realizing that...

I am blind.

Staring down at the desk, I realize with a sudden sense of shock that I can see absolutely nothing. I can hear footsteps in the basement, and a moment later I hear a voice howling somewhere in the house, calling out the name Delilah over and over again. I suppose that Jack has found what is left of Delilah's body, although this is not possible since Jack is not real. Besides, I dumped most of the woman's carcass far from here.

Or did I?

Was even that an illusion? I no longer know what is real and what is not, and I feel that this uncertainty is tipping me closer to the edge of absolute madness.

And I am blind.

I rub my eyes against the back of my hand, but this does not help.

I can see absolutely nothing, and after a moment I touch my eyes with my fingertips and feel that there is a great deal of damage. I knew that dust had begun to collect on my eyeballs, but now I feel other debris too,

along with thick and heavy scratches.
    How am I to work, if I cannot see?

CHAPTER EIGHTEEN
MADDIE

Today

"NO!" I SCREAM, pulling back and slamming the bedroom door shut, before hurrying over and grabbing the end of the dresser. Pulling the whole thing across the room, I place it in front of the door, but I know it won't be enough.

I take a step back, filled with panic, and then I turn to Matt.

"We have to -"

Suddenly I see that he's gone. There's a large patch of blood on the floor, in the exact spot where I found him earlier, but there's no sign of him at all. I look around the room, then I peer under the bed, but he's nowhere to be seen. For a moment, none of this seems possible, and I start to wonder whether I'm completely losing my mind.

"Maddie!"

Suddenly Nick bangs on the door from the other side, and I spin around just in time to see him trying the handle. Lunging at the dresser, I push it hard against the door to make sure that Nick has no chance of getting through. I can feel him trying, but a moment later he stops.

"What are you going to do now?" he asks, sounding amused by my struggles. "You're cornered, little girl. There's nowhere left to run."

"You killed her!" I sob. "You murdered her in cold blood!"

"She knew what was coming," he replies. "The moment she decided to betray me, she knew what'd happen. It's a shame, 'cause I liked her, but I guess these things happen."

"You're a monster!" I yell.

"I'll take that as a compliment," he continues, and I can tell that he's laughing now. "I knew I couldn't rely on Alex. She was a nice girl, but she was *so* changeable. Seriously, I could barely keep track of her from one moment to the next. She was always changing her mind about things. One second she was whacking you around the face and knocking you out, Maddie, and the next she was trying to help you escape. If you ask me, it was all rooted in her low self-esteem and -"

"Help!" I scream, keeping my body pressed against the dresser as I turn and look toward the window. "Somebody help me!"

"You can shout all you want," Nick replies, "but no-one's going to come. Haven't you noticed something about this house, Maddie? It has a real knack for keeping its secrets to itself. I guess maybe it's just had a lot of practice. There's a real energy about the place, a really weird vibe that's hard to pin down."

"Help me!" I shout, sobbing now as I try to think of some way out. "Please, somebody..."

"You just keep on making bad decisions," Nick continues, and I can feel him trying to door again. "I thought you were smart, Maddie, but now it's starting to look like you're just another idiot. That's gotta hurt, right? I mean, the average person would probably not have gotten herself into this mess. And let's be honest, you could have been out of here by now. It takes a special kind of stupid to end up in the mess you're in right now."

"Help me!" I cry out, although my voice is cracking as tears stream down my face. "Matt! Run! Matt, get out of here!"

I slump down to the floor, while still pressing my body against the dresser. I have to get out of here, I have to save Matt even if I don't manage to get myself out of here.

"Matt?" Nick says after a moment. "Well, that's interesting. Your buddy Matt was supposed to be there in the room with you, Maddie. But if you're calling out and telling him to run, I get the feeling he's maybe not where he oughta be. Thanks for letting me know."

"No!" I yell, turning and looking at the door handle as I hear Nick stepping away. "Don't hurt him! Don't you dare hurt him!"

I wait, but Nick's footsteps have already reached

the other bedroom door.

"Hello?" I hear him call out. "Anybody in here? I know you didn't make it downstairs, Matty-boy, so that means you're still up here somewhere. Are you awake? Did you drag your broken body somewhere to hide, hoping your little girlfriend'd save the day? Unfortunately, it doesn't matter *where* you're hiding, 'cause I'll find you. You see, your friend opened her big mouth and let me know that you're not where I left you. You can thank her for that as you die. She really *is* a stupid little bitch, isn't she?"

"Matt, run!" I shout, but deep down I know that there's no way he has the strength to get out of here. He must be hiding somewhere in one of the upstairs rooms, with only the knife for defense. "I'm sorry," I sob, realizing that it's my fault yet again. "I'm sorry, Matt. I let you down."

I have to help him.

I can still hear Nick calling out, taunting him, but I can't just sit here and wait. If I don't do anything, Nick'll find him and kill him, and then he'll come for me. If I stay here on the floor, shivering and terrified, I'll die anyway. Matt and I will both die.

If I'm going to get killed, I might as well go down fighting.

Getting to my feet, I start dragging the dresser out of the way. I know Nick can probably hear what I'm doing, but right now all I can think about is that I have to at least *try* to save Matt. My hands are shaking, but I get the dresser out of the way and then I pull the door open. Who knows? Maybe I'll get lucky.

Stepping out onto the landing, I see open doors but no sign of Nick.

"Where are you?" I whisper, but my voice is too low to be heard. "Where are you?" I call out again, and this time I know Nick must be able to hear me. "Come on, you coward! Show yourself!"

I wait, but all I hear is silence. I swear, it's almost as if Nick vanished into thin air.

"I know you're here," I continue, taking a step forward, poised to defend myself if he comes rushing at me from one of the rooms. I don't have a plan, but plans haven't helped me very much so far. "Is this some kind of game?"

Stopping, I look around again, and then I see the top of the stairs. I could run and get help, but then I'd be leaving Matt behind to face certain death. I know Matt would tell me to get out of here, but deep down I also know that there's no way I can do that. We're way beyond the point where fetching help is an option. Besides, I'm sure Nick expects me to try running, and he'll come after me. For the first time in my life, I'm going to do the right thing. The element of surprise might even help me. I've got to fight.

First, though, I need a weapon.

Backing against the wall, I look around for something that I might be able to use. Spotting nothing, however, I finally hurry over to the banister. I pull on one of the rotten rails, and sure enough I find that it's a little loose. Kicking the bottom, I manage to break the wood, and after a moment I pull the rail out and hold it up. Sure enough, the broken end looks pretty sharp. Not as sharp as a knife, of course, but I might still be able to use it to defend myself. If I'm going down, I'm taking Nick with me.

"I'm coming, Matt," I whisper, as I turn and look at the open doors. "I'll find you."

I know he's in one of those rooms, but I don't understand why Nick is being so quiet. I guess he's waiting for me to make my move, and I'm sure he thinks he'll be able to drop me easily enough. Alex fought back against him, and she paid the ultimate price. I'm not exactly much of a fighter, but I figure I at least have a shot. In fact, I have *more* than a shot. As I adjust my grip on the broken railing, I tell myself that as soon as I see Nick I'll drive the splintered end into his gut and do the same thing to him that he did to Alex. I never thought I could hurt another human being, but right now I'm absolutely certain that I can fight back against this bastard.

Finally, cautiously, I start making my way toward one of the open doors. The only sound I hear is my own footsteps, and I know Nick has to be close, but I'm ready. When he comes for me, I'll -

Suddenly I spot movement to my left. I turn and lash out with the railing, but I lose my grip and simply hit the side of the nearest door as the wood falls from my hand. At the same time, Nick lunges at me and flashes his knife in my direction, and I let out a cry as I feel a sharp pain slicing deep through my belly.

CHAPTER NINETEEN
DOCTOR CHARLES GRAZIER

Thursday October 4th, 1888

"WHERE IS THE CHILD?"

I can hear the sound of a cart being driven along the street outside.

"Where is the child?"

In the distance, somebody shouts.

"Where is the child?"

"Where is *what* child?" I ask finally, sitting at my desk and trying to focus on the confession that I'm writing. I've been trying to ignore the voice, but now I am unable to help myself. I cannot see, of course, but I suppose that perhaps my sight will return if I wait. "If you mean Catherine, I -"

"Where is Delilah's child?" Jack continues, his voice tense with some emotion or another. Anger, maybe, or fear.

It's difficult to tell when one is dealing with such a brute. And that is what Jack is, a -

"WHERE IS DELILAH'S CHILD?" he roars, before storming to the desk and slamming his fists against the top with such force that my lamp shudders. All of this I hear, rather than see. "You will tell me right now what you've done with the child you cut from her belly!"

"Will I?" I ask, raising a skeptical, amused eyebrow. "And whatever makes you believe that?"

"Because if you do not," he continues breathlessly, "I swear by any gods that happen to be watching, I will force the information out of you, and I will ensure that your confession is your dying breath! You miserable -"

Suddenly I burst out laughing. Not in an attempt to embarrass the poor fellow, of course, but simply because I find him so utterly preposterous. Here he is, in my home, attempting to threaten me. Of course, he is not without his strength, so after a moment – still chuckling – I open the drawer on the desk's right-hand side and take out one of my sharper letter-openers. Indeed, I am quite impressed by my ability to do this while I am blinded, and I can only suppose that once again my natural talents are making themselves evident.

It no longer matters whether or not Jack is real. I am blind, so how am I to tell?

"Do you think this is amusing?" he asks. "You once told me that killing a child was a line you could never cross, Doctor Grazier, and now look at you. Tell me what you've done with Delilah's baby."

I tilt my head and look toward him. Or rather, I look toward where I suppose he must be. Does he know yet that I am blind? As I tighten my grip on the letter-opener, I remind myself that although I am sure Jack is not real, I might yet have need to defend myself. After all, it is possible that...

Wait.

Why must I defend myself?

He is an illusion, a waking dream.

"You don't really want me to tell you about the child," I say finally. "Deep down, you can guess what I did, and the truth is most likely even worse than you imagine. If I were to tell you the details, if I told you how I the child to help Catherine, your paltry little mind would no doubt snap. Believe me, Jack, it is much better for you not to know, but if you insist on being told, I can take you down to the basement and show you the various jars and pipettes and tubes that contain the answer. I can show you the unwashed blades." I wait for a reply, but he seems dumbstruck. "Would you like that?" I ask, and then I get to my feet. "Shall we go now?"

Again I wait, and for a moment the room fills with silence.

"Is it dead?" he asks finally.

"The baby?" I pause, before nodding. "Yes, it is dead."

"You killed it?"

"I did."

"Did it die while it was being removed from Delilah, or did it last any time at all after that point?"

"There were some signs of life for a few

minutes," I explain, "as I took it over to the counter so that I could... Oh, but you don't want to know the details, do you? You don't want to know exactly how I used the child's body. You have an imagination, do you not? So use it. Imagine the worst thing I could possibly have done with that child, and then know that the truth is so much more awful."

"May the Lord have mercy on your soul," he replies, mimicking the sound of a man with real emotions. "You have done the one thing that I thought was beyond you."

"Then you underestimated me," I tell him. "That is understandable. Anything I might have said earlier is a moot point now. I needed the child's body, so I took it. Why should a great man be denied the chance to complete his work, simply because society insists that a weak little child is so important? What would it have become in life, anyway? A solicitor? A clerk? A doctor?" At this, I cannot contain a slight chuckle. "This world is already far too full. I should be praised for helping with the overpopulation problem."

"You murdered that baby," he sneers.

"I did what I had to do. For Catherine. For love. And truth be told, I am confident that my plan was rooted in good ideas. I do not know why certain failings occurred, but you cannot deny that I raised her body from the dead." I pause, wondering just how much to tell him, but then I remember that I have the letter-opener for protection. "The child's blood was key," I add. "A child is pure and unsullied by the world, so naturally its blood is far more potent. I regret the action that I had to take, but one must not get maudlin about these things. The fresh blood gave her some extra strength, although still the mind is -"

"You murdered Delilah!" he spits.

"She was a resource to be used, as was the child." I can't help smiling again, amused by his pathetic attempt to sound like a moral man. "You come from the streets, Jack," I continue. "You know how life works. The weak are eaten up by the living, and in this case I deemed it necessary to use Delilah and her unborn child in order to save Catherine. Let us not perform some pantomime of emotion and pretend that this was the wrong choice, because -"

Suddenly I hear his footsteps coming around the table. I take a step back and instinctively raise the letter-opener, although after a moment I bump against the wall.

He is not real.

I must remember that.

He cannot interfere. I shall finish my confession, and then I shall burn this house to the ground, and I shall cut my wrists in the flames.

"Come any closer," I say firmly, "and I'll gut you!"

"You wouldn't know *how*," he replies, putting on a good show as he pretends to be angry. "You only kill women, and children. You wouldn't stand a chance against anyone who can actually fight back."

"Oh wouldn't I?" I ask, unable to stifle a grin. "Delilah fought back, or at least she tried. Tell me, Jack, when you attack a man, do you simply try to pummel him into submission? Of course you do, whereas I am an expert on human anatomy. Why, I know exactly where to strike you with this blade, and how to incapacitate you without even breaking a sweat. You can't seriously think that I let you have free roam in my house, without knowing precisely how to kill you. I could have ended your life at any time."

"I dare you to try!" he barks. "Besides, it is clear that you cannot see."

"Come at me then, man," I reply, raising the letter-opener a little higher. "You will be dead inside of thirty seconds!"

"I swear -"

"Remember who you are!" I shout angrily. "Remember *what* you are! You are a beast, you are a guest in my home and you serve *me*! The fact that you can walk on two legs is a miracle, let alone the fact that you are able to comport yourself in the rough approximation of a gentleman. Make no mistake, however... You are a wretched creature, and while you might convince yourself that you feel true emotions, you actually feel nothing of the sort. You are a miserable, filthy beast and you will get down on your knees and beg for your life!"

I wait for him to do as he is told. I shall not spare him, of course. I intend merely to make him kneel so that I can more easily cut his throat. For too long, I have endured his presence. Now that I have finally found a way to cure Catherine and bring her back, I have no need of this pathetic cur and it is time to put him out of his misery. This shall be my final gift to the world. And yet...

And yet I can make no sense of this. One moment I am determined to live, the next I wish to die; one moment I still believe that I can save Catherine, and the next I am certain she is lost forever. It is as if my mind can no longer settle on any one particular idea, leaving me lost in a mess of confusion and fear. I steady myself a little and try to draw my thoughts together, but I am concerned that I shall never truly be myself again. If any man can taste this degree of madness and then return to sanity, it is I, yet I fear now that sanity is beyond me.

Do I want to live?

Do I want to die?

All I know, at this moment, is that Jack must go.

"Kneel!" I say finally. "Kneel or I will cut you down where you stand."

"Try," he replies.

"Don't be foolish!" I shout. "Kneel, man! Kneel and -"

Before I can finish, I realize that I am dribbling. I reach up and wipe saliva from my chin. I know not why I have become akin to a slathering beast, but more and more liquid is running from my mouth.

"Kneel!" I say again, forcing a grin to hide the fact that I am in distress. "Kneel, you damnable cur, and face your proper punishment! KNEEL!"

"Never! Not to you!"

"Kneel, I -"

***

DOCTOR CHARLES GRAZIER

Blood rushes between my fingers. There is so much blood, I can smell it in the air.

***

The memory flashed into my thoughts, for just a moment. I remembered being down in the basement, cutting Delilah Culpepper open and removing her child. In truth, these memories have been flashing unbidden into my mind all day, as if they are trying to compete with my conscious thoughts.

"You murdered Delilah!" Jack sneers.

Unable to stifle a laugh, I realize that I must go to him. Still, it is inconceivable that a gentleman could be injured by such a brute in his own home, and I know exactly where to strike him. I take a moment to consider my aim, and to concoct a plan by which I shall fool him with a dummy move, and at the same time I try to meet his dull, foolish gaze. He must be standing directly in front of me, must he not?

"If you insist, then," I say with a smile. "Prepare to meet your maker. Or sink into the depths of damnation. After all, that is where you come from, is it not? From hell? So go back there!"

And with that, I strike, slicing at his throat with the blade. Somehow I miss, but I go to strike again, only for him to grab my arm and crack it against his knee. I let out a cry of pain and drop the letter-opener, and then I am shoved rudely back against the desk. All of this occurs in the darkness of my own blindness.

Dropping to my knees, I reach down to touch my arm, only to find that the pain is too intense. The brute has snapped the bone clean in two.

"Curse you!" I stammer, wincing with pain as I try and fail to clench my right fist. "You will pay for that!"

"*I* will pay?" Jack asks, stepping over to the fireplace and – I believe, from the sound alone – picking up one of the pokers. "Perhaps I have seen enough of your work, Doctor Charles Grazier. Perhaps I can succeed where you did not."

"You?" I splutter, taking a moment to summon the strength I shall need when I try to stand. "Get down here so that I can finish you off! Or are you not even real? Perhaps you are like Sanderson, you are just an illusion. No, wait, I saw you talking to Delilah Culpepper. Well, maybe that was an illusion too. Maybe there's no way to tell anymore."

"You killed Delilah," he replies, stepping closer, "but I will not let her go. She is a beautiful, perfect creature, and perhaps some good can come of your work if I am able to bring her back."

"You really believe that, don't you?" I say with a chuckle. "Oh your poor, pathetic, deluded little -"

Suddenly the poker crashes against the side of my head, striking me just above the left eye. I feel my skull collapse, and a bright flash briefly fills my eyes as I drop down against the ground. Reaching up to protect my face, I am just about to cry out when the poker crashes down against me yet again, this time shattering my hands and causing me to let out an agonized scream.

***

I drop the child into a small metal dish, and then I lick the blood from my fingers.

***

I roll onto my back, and after a moment I manage by some miracle to see a little out of my right eye.

Jack swings the poker at me again, crushing the top of my skull. Now I am blinded for good, and I taste a blood-filled, gurgling cry as it erupts from my lips. Within seconds, however, the poker strikes my head again, then again and again, then yet more times with increasing force. I hear Jack cry out, too, as if he is finally giving into his animal side. And still he beats me, until I can feel sections of my skull being quite knocked away to expose the brain beneath.

***

The blood tastes so vital. So powerful. How can it fail to revive Catherine?

***

"You're not real!" I gasp, although I'm not sure whether the words are coming out. "You're not real! You can't be real!"

"Perhaps *this*," he snarls, "will persuade you

otherwise."

A moment later, I feel the full force of his boot smashing through my face and into my brain, even bursting out through the back. My jaw still works, however, and I am just about able to cry out at him in furious defiance.

"You're not real! You're not real! You're not -"

CHAPTER TWENTY
MADDIE

Today

"NICE TRY," Nick says as I slump back against the wall. "No cigar, but very nice try."

Whimpering with pain, I reach down and see that blood is starting to soak the front of my shirt. Nick's blade sliced straight through the fabric and into my belly, and all I can manage is to press my hands against the wound. A moment later, however, I realize I can feel something starting to force its way out through the bloodied slit, as if my guts are trying to burst through. There's blood, too; so much blood, I can feel it running between my fingers and soaking my shirt all the way through.

This can't be happening.

Please, let it all be a dream.

"That was a pretty neat cut, wasn't it?" he

continues, taking a step toward me with the knife still in his hand. His eyes look so dark now, almost devoid of human life. Almost dead. "I even impressed *myself* with that one. Come on, the game's up now, Maddie. Let go. Let's see what happens when you let nature take its course."

"Go to hell!" I sob, but I can still feel my intestines trying to come out from my belly, and I'm starting to tremble as rich, pulsing pain fills my mind. I want to run, but I don't think I have the strength.

"At least you put up more of a fight than Alex," he continues with a grin. "Don't worry, Maddie. I'm going to use you for an experiment. I'm going to take out your organs one by one. You can even watch for a while, if you like. It'll be a kind of anatomical experiment, something to keep me occupied until the others arrive. Did I mention the others? They're gonna treat me like royalty when they find out what I've discovered here in this house. I think I was guided here. I think the great lord Jack the Ripper himself wanted *me* to be the one who uncovered his true identity. The name Charles Grazier is gonna live in history. I might even try to summon his ghost, so I can present myself to him as the one who finally gave him the glory he wanted."

I try to cry out, but the pain is intense and I can already taste blood in the back of my mouth. I try yet again, but this time all I manage is to spray some blood-laced saliva down my chin.

"You're so lucky," Nick says, stepping closer and raising the knife. "When I write the history of our movement, your name -"

Suddenly something slams into him from behind. Screaming, I duck out of the way as he slumps against the wall, and his knife misses my face by less than an inch. Turning, I'm just in time to see Matt lunging at him again, trying to drive his blade into Nick's shoulder. At the last moment, however, Nick slams his elbow into Matt's face, knocking him back.

I grab Nick's leg, hoping to slow him down so that Matt can try again. Instead, however, Nick simply slams my head against the wall, and I cry out as I drop to the ground. Still clutching my belly, I feel a jolt of pain run through my chest, and then I look up just as Nick hauls Matt to his feet and shoves him back.

"Leave him alone!" I gasp.

"You're a feisty one," Nick sneers, kicking Matt in the face and knocking him into one of the bedrooms, before stepping through after him. "What am I gonna do with you, huh?"

"Maddie, run!" Matt shouts, turning to me. "Maddie, get out of here!"

"Matt!" I yell, but suddenly the door slams shut and a moment later I hear a gurgled shout from the other side. I stumble to the door and try to push it open, but Nick must have locked it from the other side. I hesitate for a moment, still clutching my belly, and then I realize that my only chance is to get out of here and call for help. At the same time, I've lost so much blood that I'm starting to feel weak, and for a moment I can't even remember how I got here.

"Matt," I whisper. "Alex..."

I wince as the pain hits harder.

"Alex!" I shout, hoping against hope that she'll come and help. "Alex, please..."

And then I remember.

In my mind's eye, I see her dying face as she was shoved down the steps that lead to the basement. Even now, that memory is already fading again, and I can barely remember my own name. Blood is flowing from my wound, and I'm starting to feel light-headed. Turning, I start stumbling along the landing. I manage a couple of steps but then suddenly I fall, tripping on a loose floorboard and dropping to my knees. I let out a cry of pain as I tumble forward, but somehow I manage to keep my hands clamped tight against my bloodied belly.

"Matt!" I scream, trying to get to my feet but not quite summoning the strength. "Matt, run! Get out of -"

Before I can finish, I cry out in pain as more blood spills from my belly and runs between my fingers. The pain is intense, filling my mind for a few seconds as my knees buckle under my weight. I start slipping down, but somehow I manage to drag myself up.

"Matt, run!" I gasp, tasting blood in my mouth now. "Matt, you have to get out of here."

Wait.

Matt.

Where's Matt?

I lean against the wall for a moment and look down at my clasped hands. The cut on my belly runs all the way from one side to the other, and I can feel the weight of my intestines pushing to get out. If I move my hands away, the torn flesh will split all the way and there'll be nothing holding my guts in place. Even now, I can feel more blood seeping out between my fingers, and I think I can even see a sliver of glistening redness pushing against the cut from deep inside. And no matter how hard I try to stay up, I can't keep from sliding down once again toward the floorboards.

I adjust my hands a little, hoping to get a better grip, but the pain is intense and my fingers are covered in blood. I feel nauseous too, as if my shifting guts are trying to expel everything they contain. My underwear's soaked too. Even if I get out of here, I don't know how -

And then suddenly I hear him.

I freeze.

I don't dare look, but I know he's close.

Who? Someone. It's all a jumble.

Letting out a groan of pain, I try again to get to my feet. This time I force myself up, but I can feel my knees trembling as if they might buckle again at any moment. I start stumbling forward, heading unsteadily toward the top of the stairs while leaning heavily against the wall. With each step, more and more blood is forced out through the cut in my belly, and when I get to the top of the stairs I let out a whimpered sob. Each step feels as if it has to be my last, yet somehow I've made it this far. I've slipped in my own blood and I've almost passed out as pain bursts through my body, but I refuse to curl up and die. I have to fight.

"Matt!" I gasp. "He's here! Run!"

I don't know where Matt is right now, but I have to find him. If he's hurt – if that monster has gotten to him – I have to make sure he's okay and get him out of here. If anything's happened to Matt, I'll never forgive myself.

I pause for a moment, leaning against the wall and letting out another groan, but then I hear a bumping sound. This time I turn instinctively, and to my horror I see the silhouette of a man standing at the far end of the landing. He's facing this way, and in his right hand he's holding a large knife with a curved blade. Even from here, I can see that blood is dribbling down onto the floorboards.

My name is Maddie Harper, and I am not going to die like this.

"You're not going to get me," I whisper, trying to find some strength from somewhere. "I won't let you."

I lunge at the table next to the top of the stairs, desperately trying to find something I can use as a weapon. I miss the table, however, and slam against the wall, and my hands barely contain the sloughing mess that's threatening to come slopping out of my belly at any moment. I feel dizzy, and it takes a moment before I can even turn and focus on the silhouetted figure.

"Leave me alone!" I scream. "Go to hell!"

Suddenly he takes a step toward me, and he emerges from the shadows enough for me to see his dark, dead eyes. I recognize him, he...

I have to get out of here.

Gripped by panic, I turn and start making my way down the stairs, but I immediately slip. I try to steady myself against the wall, but I quickly realize that I'm starting to fall. As I tumble forward, I instinctively reach out to grab the banister, almost but not quite managing to save myself. Finally I scream as I fall. My remaining hand slips down and my intestines burst out from my belly, splattering against the bare wooden steps.

CHAPTER TWENTY-ONE
"DOCTOR CHARLES GRAZIER"

Thursday October 4th, 1888

"YOU'RE NOT REAL! You're not real! You're not -"

His final cry becomes a faint gurgle, as I stamp my boot straight through his skull. Blood splatters against the wall, and I twist my heel against fragments of shattered bone before taking a step back. Grazier's left hand twitches slightly, as if there is yet some spark of life in his body, but then finally he falls entirely still.

***

Despite having never touched one before, I am nevertheless able to tie the bow-tie that I slipped from Doctor Grazier's neck. Indeed, as I stand in the study and look at myself in the mirror, I rather believe that I have done a good job.

I am wearing the man's clothes, and – apart from some dirt on my face, which will come off easily enough with a swift wash – I am astounded to see that I look like a gentleman. A real, proper gentleman, of the type that I used to watch when I was younger. As a child, I'd hide in bushes in the smarter parts of London and watch as rich people walked past, and I used to daydream about what it would be like if I could become like them. I dreamed of success for a while, before eventually realizing that I could not work my way up from poverty. But now...

Now, standing here in Doctor Grazier's clothes, I look like a real gentleman. Indeed, I doubt that anyone would be able to tell that I was not born into this kind of clothing.

"You're not real!"

That's what poor Doctor Grazier shouted at me as he died. His voice was gurgling with blood, a little more with each word, until finally the heel of my boot knocked his jawbone clean away. Looking down, I see that there is still a great deal of his blood splattered against the wall. He tried to put up a fight, but it seemed that he was quite insane by the time I found him today. It seems that as he died, Doctor Grazier believed that I was somehow a figment of his imagination. I suppose he did not believe that he was truly going to die.

Then again, in one way he did *not* die. For although the man's body is wrecked and bloodied on the floor, I intend to take on his attributes to the greatest possible extent. I studied him extensively over the past week, watching his mannerisms and trying to understand how his mind works, and now I believe that I shall be able to *become* him. By so doing, I shall transcend my old life on the streets, and I shall become a proper gentleman. I shall also succeed where he failed.

I shall bring my sweet love back to life.

"I am Doctor Charles Grazier," I say out loud, although I can instantly tell that my voice is all wrong. Growing up on the streets, I developed a certain way of speaking, and I suppose it will take time to appropriate Doctor Grazier's more refined ones. "I am Doctor Charles Grazier," I say again, and I believe there is already a slightly improvement. "I am Doctor Charles Grazier. *I* am Doctor Charles Grazier."

Those words sound so foolish coming from my lips. A gentleman speaks with a refined tone, and I cannot subdue my street-born accent. Still, I have time to work on such things.

After a moment I turn and look across the room, and I see the naked, bloated body on the floor, with its head smashed to pieces and blood having splattered several meters in every direction. There is even blood on the poker I used to kill the man, which rests in a patch of crimson. I had hoped to kill him with my bare hands, but a brief moment of pure rage overtook me. I am calmer now, however, since I know that gentleman are always calm.

"I am Doctor Charles Grazier," I whisper, before stepping over to the body and using my right foot to roll him onto his back. "*I* am Doctor Charles Grazier," I continue. "I am *now*, at least. How does it feel, old man, to have your very name and life usurped?"

His dead face stares up at me. Or what is left of

his face, at least. He might have kept himself together in life, and affected a certain degree of class, but in death he wears the same gormless idiocy that I saw many times during my time in the city's rougher parts. As it turns out, a dead gentleman looks very much like a dead thief. Perhaps all men, having suffered a violent death, ultimately look more or less like this. Perhaps death levels us all.

"You knew me as Jack," I say after a moment, even though I know the old man cannot possibly hear me, "but now I think I shall take on aspects of your life. I shall become you, so that I can continue your work and bring Delilah back."

Then again, maybe he *can* hear me.

Maybe he is somewhere around, still insane but now a ghost.

Maybe he screams in some distant void, begging to come back to the world.

Reaching down, I pick up the poker and use it to gently bump the side of his face. He does not respond, of course, since he cannot. Doctor Charles Grazier is dead, his head having been crushed from behind to a pulp, yet I have risen to take his place. If I gave any thought whatsoever to the concept of fate, I think I would believe that this moment had been my destiny ever since I first spotted him in one of the city's dark alleys.

"I shall continue your work," I tell him, "albeit in a more improving fashion." I pause for a moment, before realizing that there is another task to complete before I can go back down to the basement. "First, though, I think I know the most fitting manner in which to dispose of your corpse."

Taking hold of his ankles, I start dragging him out toward the hallway. His shattered head leaves a thick trail of blood on the floor, but that matters not: I can clean the mess up later. For now, I simply have to get his corpse out of here and then get on with the task of saving Delilah.

I can do this. I am Doctor Charles Grazier now.

DOCTOR CHARLES GRAZIER

Coming Soon

THE RAVEN WATCHER

(THE HOUSE OF JACK THE RIPPER BOOK 7)

Trapped alone with a murderer, Maddie desperately tries to find a way out of the house.

Meanwhile, a century earlier, Jack begins to follow Doctor Grazier's plans, although he soon finds that his mind is crumbling.

Books in this series

Broken Window
In Darkness Dwell
Cradle to Grave
The Lady Screams
A Beast Well Tamed
Doctor Charles Grazier

Coming soon

The Raven Catcher
The Final Act

Also by Amy Cross

The Soul Auction

"I saw a woman on the beach. I watched her face a demon."

Thirty years after her mother's death, Alice Ashcroft is drawn back to the coastal English town of Curridge. Somebody in Curridge has been reviewing Alice's novels online, and in those reviews there have been tantalizing hints at a hidden truth. A truth that seems to be linked to her dead mother.

"Thirty years ago, there was a soul auction."

Once she reaches Curridge, Alice finds strange things happening all around her. Something attacks her car. A figure watches her on the beach at night. And when she tries to find the person who has been reviewing her books, she makes a horrific discovery.

What really happened to Alice's mother thirty years ago? Who was she talking to, just moments before dropping dead on the beach? What caused a huge rockfall that nearly tore a nearby cliff-face in half? And what sinister presence is lurking in the grounds of the local church?

Also by Amy Cross

Darper Danver: The Complete First Series

Five years ago, three friends went to a remote cabin in the woods and tried to contact the spirit of a long-dead soldier. They thought they could control whatever happened next. They were wrong...

Newly released from prison, Cassie Briggs returns to Fort Powell, determined to get her life back on track. Soon, however, she begins to suspect that an ancient evil still lurks in the nearby cabin. Was the mysterious Darper Danver really destroyed all those years ago, or does her spirit still linger, waiting for a chance to return?

As Cassie and her ex-boyfriend Fisher are finally forced to face the truth about what happened in the cabin, they realize that Darper isn't ready to let go of their lives just yet. Meanwhile, a vengeful woman plots revenge for her brother's murder, and a New York ghost writer arrives in town to uncover the truth. Before long, strange carvings begin to appear around town and blood starts to flow once again.

Also by Amy Cross

The Ghost of Molly Holt

"Molly Holt is dead. There's nothing to fear in this house."

When three teenagers set out to explore an abandoned house in the middle of a forest, they think they've found the location where the infamous Molly Holt video was filmed.

They've found much more than that...

Tim doesn't believe in ghosts, but he has a crush on a girl who does. That's why he ends up taking her out to the house, and it's also why he lets her take his only flashlight. But as they explore the house together, Tim and Becky start to realize that something else might be lurking in the shadows.

Something that, ten years ago, suffered unimaginable pain.

Something that won't rest until a terrible wrong has been put right.

Also by Amy Cross

American Coven

He kidnapped three women and held them in his basement. He thought they couldn't fight back. He was wrong...

Snatched from the street near her home, Holly Carter is taken to a rural house and thrown down into a stone basement. She meets two other women who have also been kidnapped, and soon Holly learns about the horrific rituals that take place in the house. Eventually, she's called upstairs to take her place in the ice bath.

As her nightmare continues, however, Holly learns about a mysterious power that exists in the basement, and which the three women might be able to harness. When they finally manage to get through the metal door, however, the women have no idea that their fight for freedom is going to stretch out for more than a decade, or that it will culminate in a final, devastating demonstration of their new-found powers.

Also by Amy Cross

The Ash House

Why would anyone ever return to a haunted house?

For Diane Mercer the answer is simple. She's dying of cancer, and she wants to know once and for all whether ghosts are real.

Heading home with her young son, Diane is determined to find out whether the stories are real. After all, everyone else claimed to see and hear strange things in the house over the years. Everyone except Diane had some kind of experience in the house, or in the little ash house in the yard.

As Diane explores the house where she grew up, however, her son is exploring the yard and the forest. And while his mother might be struggling to come to terms with her own impending death, Daniel Mercer is puzzled by fleeting appearances of a strange little girl who seems drawn to the ash house, and by strange, rasping coughs that he keeps hearing at night.

The Ash House is a horror novel about a woman who desperately wants to know what will happen to her when she dies, and about a boy who uncovers the shocking truth about a young girl's murder.

Also by Amy Cross

Haunted

Twenty years ago, the ghost of a dead little girl drove Sheriff Michael Blaine to his death.

Now, that same ghost is coming for his daughter.

Returning to the small town where she grew up, Alex Roberts is determined to live a normal, quiet life. For the residents of Railham, however, she's an unwelcome reminder of the town's darkest hour.

Twenty years ago, nine-year-old Mo Garvey was found brutally murdered in a nearby forest. Everyone thinks that Alex's father was responsible, but if the killer was brought to justice, why is the ghost of Mo Garvey still after revenge?

And how far will the real killer go to protect his secret, when Alex starts getting closer to the truth?

Haunted is a horror novel about a woman who has to face her past, about a town that would rather forget, and about a little girl who refuses to let death stand in her way.

Also by Amy Cross

The Curse of Wetherley House

"If you walk through that door, Evil Mary will get you."

When she agrees to visit a supposedly haunted house with an old friend, Rosie assumes she'll encounter nothing more scary than a few creaks and bumps in the night. Even the legend of Evil Mary doesn't put her off. After all, she knows ghosts aren't real. But when Mary makes her first appearance, Rosie realizes she might already be trapped.

For more than a century, Wetherley House has been cursed. A horrific encounter on a remote road in the late 1800's has already caused a chain of misery and pain for all those who live at the house. Wetherley House was abandoned long ago, after a terrible discovery in the basement, something has remained undetected within its room. And even the local children know that Evil Mary waits in the house for anyone foolish enough to walk through the front door.

Before long, Rosie realizes that her entire life has been defined by the spirit of a woman who died in agony. Can she become the first person to escape Evil Mary, or will she fall victim to the same fate as the house's other occupants?

Also by Amy Cross

The Ghosts of Hexley Airport

Ten years ago, more than two hundred people died in a horrific plane crash at Hexley Airport.

Today, some say their ghosts still haunt the terminal building.

When she starts her new job at the airport, working a night shift as part of the security team, Casey assumes the stories about the place can't be true. Even when she has a strange encounter in a deserted part of the departure hall, she's certain that ghosts aren't real.

Soon, however, she's forced to face the truth. Not only is there something haunting the airport's buildings and tarmac, but a sinister force is working behind the scenes to replicate the circumstances of the original accident. And as a snowstorm moves in, Hexley Airport looks set to witness yet another disaster.

Also by Amy Cross

The Girl Who Never Came Back

Twenty years ago, Charlotte Abernathy vanished while playing near her family's house. Despite a frantic search, no trace of her was found until a year later, when the little girl turned up on the doorstep with no memory of where she'd been.

Today, Charlotte has put her mysterious ordeal behind her, even though she's never learned where she was during that missing year. However, when her eight-year-old niece vanishes in similar circumstances, a fully-grown Charlotte is forced to make a fresh attempt to uncover the truth.

Originally published in 2013, the fully revised and updated version of *The Girl Who Never Came Back* tells the harrowing story of a woman who thought she could forget her past, and of a little girl caught in the tangled web of a dark family secret.

Also by Amy Cross

The Devil, the Witch and the Whore
(The Deal book 1)

"Leave the forest alone. Whatever's out there, just let it be. Don't make it angry."

When a horrific discovery is made at the edge of town, Sheriff James Kopperud realizes the answers he seeks might be waiting beyond in the vast forest. But everybody in the town of Deal knows that there's something out there in the forest, something that should never be disturbed. A deal was made long ago, a deal that was supposed to keep the town safe. And if he insists on investigating the murder of a local girl, James is going to have to break that deal and head out into the wilderness.

Meanwhile, James has no idea that his estranged daughter Ramsey has returned to town. Ramsey is running from something, and she thinks she can find safety in the vast tunnel system that runs beneath the forest. Before long, however, Ramsey finds herself coming face to face with creatures that hide in the shadows. One of these creatures is known as the devil, and another is known as the witch. They're both waiting for the whore to arrive, but for very different reasons. And soon Ramsey is offered a terrible deal, one that could save or destroy the entire town, and maybe even the world.

Also by Amy Cross

Asylum
(The Asylum Trilogy book 1)

"No-one ever leaves Lakehurst. The staff, the patients, the ghosts... Once you're here, you're stuck forever."

After shooting her little brother dead, Annie Radford is sent to Lakehurst psychiatric hospital for assessment. Hearing voices in her head, Annie is forced to undergo experimental new treatments devised by a mysterious old man who lives in the hospital's attic. It soon becomes clear that the hospital's staff, led by the vicious Nurse Winter, are hiding something horrific at Lakehurst.

As Annie struggles to survive the hospital, she learns more about Nurse Winter's own story. Once a promising young medical student, Kirsten Winter also heard voices in her head. Voices that traveled a long way to reach her. Voices that have a plan of their own. Voices that will stop at nothing to get what they want.

What kind of signals are being transmitted from the basement of the hospital? Who is the old man in the attic? Why are living human brains kept in jars? And what is the dark secret that lurks at the heart of the hospital?

Also by Amy Cross

The Devil's Hand

"I felt it last night! I was all alone, and suddenly a hand touched my shoulder!"

The year is 1943. Beacon's Ash is a private, remote school in the North of England, and all its pupils are fallen girls. Pregnant and unmarried, they have been sent away by their families. For Ivy Jones, a young girl who arrived at the school several months earlier, Beacon's Ash is a nightmare, and her fears are strengthened when one of her classmates is killed in mysterious circumstances.

Has the ghost of Abigail Cartwright returned to the school? Who or what is responsible for the hand that touches the girls' shoulders in the dead of night? And is the school's headmaster Jeremiah Kane just a madman who seeks to cause misery, or is he in fact on the trail of the Devil himself? Soon ghosts are stalking the dark corridors, and Ivy realizes she has to face the evil that lurks in the school's shadows.

The Devil's Hand is a horror novel about a girl who seeks the truth about her friend's death, and about a madman who believes the Devil stalks the school's corridors in the run-up to Christmas.

AMY CROSS

For more information, visit:

www. amycross.com

AMY CROSS

Manufactured by Amazon.ca
Bolton, ON